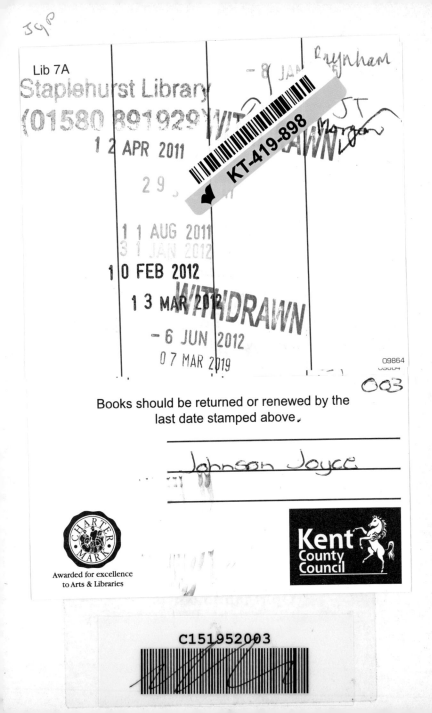

JOURNEY INTO DANGER

Ellie's new job in Canada was to be the fulfilment of a dream — she had been commissioned by Conservation Planet International to take a look at logging in British Columbia. But on arrival at Vancouver airport, Ellie's dream turned into a terrible nightmare — a hold-all containing drugs had been exchanged for her bag at Heathrow and she found herself accused of drug-smuggling. Then, the influential Rodd Pallister entered her life . . .

JOYCE JOHNSON

JOURNEY INTO DANGER

Complete and Unabridged

LINFORD
Leicester

First published in Great Britain

First Linford Edition
published 2002

British Library CIP Data

Johnson, Joyce, *1931 –*
   Journey into danger.—Large print ed.—
Linford romance library
1. Love stories
2. Large type books
 I. Title
813.5'4 [F]

ISBN 0–7089–9788–0

Published by
F. A. Thorpe (Publishing)
Anstey, Leicestershire

Set by Words & Graphics Ltd.
Anstey, Leicestershire
Printed and bound in Great Britain by
T. J. International Ltd., Padstow, Cornwall

This book is printed on acid-free paper

1

Ellie's feet were restless. Unconsciously, she shifted from one foot to the other, jogging on the spot, her excited momentum arrested by the slow questioning of the Canadian immigration officer.

He was middle-aged, with a kind, well-lived-in sort of face, and very serious. His mouth pulled down as he looked at her. Faces were her business. She imprinted them on her brain to file away for future use. This one would do nicely for a grandad in a family advert. Mentally, she sketched the contours, placed the features, noted the eye colour — and wished he'd hurry up.

Bob Burgess was to meet her, and she was already an hour late, though he, no doubt, would have noted the plane's delayed landing time on the airport information screen.

'So, you're a freelance photographer, Miss Jones?'

'Yes,' she replied impatiently.

'Just photography?'

'Some commercial art. It all depends what's needed, but you've already asked me — '

'We have to be sure. And you've come to Vancouver to work?'

Ellie sighed. Was he going to keep her there for ever? She was the only traveller left in the big hall, all the rest having been swiftly despatched. The other immigration booths were deserted. She went through her spiel again.

'I'll be based on Vancouver Island. Conservation Planet International has commissioned me. They're preparing a world-wide feature on deforestation. I'm taking a look at logging in British Columbia. All the necessary papers are there, as well as my work permit, and letters from the Forestry Commission. I'm to meet Mr Bob Burgess, a government executive, in the lobby.'

She glanced pointedly at her watch. 'I'm awfully late already — '

A look of relief on the man's face stopped her. 'At last,' he muttered, looking up, 'you've been long enough — '

Simultaneously, another voice interrupted. 'Miss Ellie Jones?' It wasn't a friendly, welcoming voice.

She spun round. Two uniformed officers had materialised at the booth, positioning themselves closely on either side of her. 'Yes, but who . . . ?'

'This is Ellie Jones.' The grandfatherly clerk shook his head sadly. 'I've held her, as you asked, but she seems OK to me.'

'I'm surprised at you, Jack. In our business, appearances can be deceptive.'

The older man wore dark glasses. Ellie thought he looked the type of man who enjoyed intimidating people. He grasped Ellie's arm tightly.

'Don't!' she cried out. 'Let me go. What are you doing?'

'Our job. We'd like you to come with

us. A few questions.'

'But why? What for? All my papers are in order. My passport . . . '

'I shouldn't argue.' The other officer, younger, softer-voiced, murmured in her ear. 'We're from customs. A problem with your luggage.'

'Luggage? I haven't reclaimed my bags yet.'

'We have them, Miss Jones. We got there before you.' They propelled her through the barrier.

'My passport — ' Ellie tried to reach back, but the clerk had gone.

'I have your passport. We'll keep it for the moment. I hope you aren't going to make a fuss.' The customs officer's tone implied he hoped she would.

Ellie's normally sunny mood was replaced by anger. The men were coldly polite, but their manner was threatening, especially the one in dark glasses. They'd no right to detain her. Ellie was confident — she'd done nothing wrong.

Her tone was sharp. 'There's no need to hang on to me. I'll come with you, but I'll expect an apology when this, whatever it is, is cleared up.'

'If we've made a mistake, we'll be glad to apologise.' The younger man moved slightly away from her.

'How long is this going to take? I was to meet Mr Burgess, from the Forestry Commission, ages ago.' If she'd hoped to impress them with one of the most respected names in Vancouver, she was disappointed.

'We've spoken to Mr Burgess. We told him you'd be delayed. He left the airport half an hour ago.'

'What?' Ellie exploded. 'How dare you? What's going on?'

'We hope you can tell us that. In here please, Miss Jones.'

They ushered her into a small, bare room containing a small table and two chairs — no windows — a fluorescent strip gave a harsh white light. Ellie gasped. Her cases were on the table! The larger was of sturdy, old-fashioned leather, bequeathed by her father, and still plastered with old travel labels. It was always unmistakable on the crowded baggage carousels, and reminded her of home and family. The other, a smaller bag, was a common, standard hold-all, which she used to carry her photographic equipment.

'I don't understand. Why are my bags here?'

'They are yours, are they? Examine them please.'

'Of course they're mine. They've got my name and address tags on.'

'Exactly.' The older officer, obviously the senior, spoke with satisfaction. 'You packed them yourself, at home in — ' He glanced at the labels. 'In Camden, North London?'

'Yes.'

'Open them, please. You have keys?'

Ellie nodded, and for the first time, a shiver of alarm slid down her spine. She took out her keys.

'The smaller one.' Dark Glasses' voice was clipped.

'That's not locked. I — er — lost the

padlock for it. My camera and lenses are in there.'

The man raised his eyebrows. 'Valuable equipment? Unsecured?'

'I suppose it is a bit foolish. It's old. I can't afford the really expensive up-to-date stuff yet.' She tried to keep the placatory tones out of her voice. She'd done nothing — there was nothing to be afraid of!

'At the beginning of your career, are you?'

The question was innocent, but there was a sneer implying something she didn't understand. Something was very wrong. Swiftly she unlocked the big case, flinging back the lid.

'It's just my clothes — personal belongings — '

'It's the other one we're interested in. Why are you refusing to do as I ask you, Miss Jones?'

'I'm not. It's just — I thought — ' She tugged at the zip of the hold-all, and frowned. 'It's stiff.' She tried again. 'This can't be my case, I've never had trouble before, mine is much easier.'

'Your name and address are on the tag. Who else's could it be? Try again.' He was unsmilling as she yanked at the zipper.

With a tearing sound, it yielded. The bag gaped open. It was stuffed with glossy magazines. Ellie picked one up, and dropped it immediately.

'Ugh!' She recoiled. 'These aren't mine. They're disgusting. Obviously some sort of mix-up. This can't be my case.'

'That's what everyone says. Sit down, please.'

'Surely you can't believe I'd have anything to do with this — this type of thing? These dreadful magazines?' She sat down, relief flooding through her. It was a ghastly mistake, but not as bad as she'd begun to fear. 'Is that it? You think I'm smuggling pornography?' Hysteria wobbled her voice. 'That's absurd. You can't possibly believe it — '

'Oh, no. That's not what we suspect.

The magazines are irrelevant — comparatively harmless erotica — but if you thought they would hide your real cargo, you don't credit us with much intelligence.' The black glasses flashed sinister, his voice cobra deadly. 'This is what we're looking for.'

He up-ended the bag, scattering its lurid contents over the table. In a swift, practised movement, he ripped out the bottom of the hold-all, thrusting the bag under her nose.

Ellie knew what she would see, but could hardly believe she'd been naïve enough not to realise where this had been leading. The officer picked up one of the bags of white powder and held it out to her.

'Drugs?' she whispered.

'Just so. At least five kilos. Do you have an explanation?'

Ellie looked at him levelly, steadying her voice. 'Yes. I've told you, the bag isn't mine. And I think I know whose it is.'

He didn't look at her, but she could

see the steely contempt and disbelief in his eyes, as he took a cassette recorder from the table drawer, placed it before her, and switched it on. His tone was flat, expressionless.

'Senior Officer Gus Henderson and colleague, Officer Tony Brent. Interviewee, Miss Ellie Jones, Camden, London, England. Room 2A, seventeen hundred hours, Vancouver Airport . . . '

Ellie put her hands to her ears, squeezed her eyes shut, and focused on the face at Heathrow. It only took seconds, it was so recent. She'd got him! In the silence, she opened her eyes. Officer Henderson was staring at her.

'I asked you a question. Why don't you answer? Do you understand the serious situation you're in? Possession of an illegal substance — '

'I do, I do. Can I telephone England? Shouldn't I have a lawyer? It's not mine. You have to believe me.' Her large, hazel eyes, intent, distressed, held his. He neither blinked, nor answered.

Ellie went on, 'I met this man at Heathrow, before we checked in. He was upset, almost in tears. He'd never been abroad before, didn't seem to know what to do. His wife had recently died, and he was visiting his daughter in Vancouver. We were catching the same plane. I got him some tea — I left him looking after my bags. I never dreamed anything like this would happen — '

'Of course not.' Officer Henderson leaned back in his chair, fractionally raising his eyebrows at the younger officer standing by the door.

Ellie flushed. 'I know it sounds implausible, but it's true. I remember now — this hold-all was the same as mine. There are hundreds of them.'

'This 'distressed' gentleman, he travelled with you on the plane? You didn't, by any chance, get his name and address?' His tone implied utter disbelief. 'And can you positively identify him?'

'I didn't see him on the plane, but it was a 747 — hundreds of passengers.'

'The departure lounge? After check-in?'

'No. I — we'd left it rather late. The passengers were boarding as I reached the gate. I just assumed he was there somewhere.'

'We'll check the passenger list.' Officer Brent spoke from across the room, and Ellie gave him a grateful look. At least his manner wasn't as acerbic as his superior's.

'Arthur Smith, he said his name was — and I've got his daughter's telephone number. In Burnaby, he said . . . '

She tailed off. Arthur Smith had told her a number of things, but now she was beginning to doubt the truth of any of them. She recalled, all too clearly now, how he'd opted for a shorter check-in queue. Busy shepherding her luggage, she'd turned round, and he'd gone. She presumed into the departure lounge. The nightmare was assuming a terrible reality.

'He has my bag, and he could simply have walked away.'

Officer Brent punched the number she'd given him, but Ellie knew in her heart that it was no use. He looked grave.

'I see. Sorry to have troubled you, ma'am. A routine check.' He replaced the handset. 'Arnie's Flower Bower! No daughter. No Arthur Smith.'

'I can draw him. I always carry a sketch pad.' She rummaged in her handbag. 'Here — '

'I'm afraid you're wasting our time, Miss Jones. You've been found in possession of a large quantity of drugs, and you'll be charged, after being searched by a woman officer. You're allowed two phone calls — '

'I haven't any drugs, I swear it.'

'Of course. Perhaps, if you'd cooperate with us — the names of your suppliers — '

Ellie could bear it no longer, and, control slipping, she shouted, 'You must let me draw him. He does exist. Don't you see, he switched bags. It was so easy for him. All I ask is a chance to convince you that there is an Arthur Smith — '

'You're making things worse, Miss — '

The door opened, and a new, resonant voice cut the air. 'What on earth is going on here? Gus? Tony? What's all the commotion?'

The stranger was tall, broad-shouldered, lean-bodied. His face, with well defined features and firm jawline, was tanned, suggesting hours spent out of doors. His curving mouth tightened as he took in the scene. The young girl with long, dishevelled, blonde hair had fear and panic in her hazel eyes. His cool, grey eyes lost their quizzically amused expression and became steel shards, as he saw the drugs on the table.

'Yet another one? Well done, Gus.' Picking up one of the white packets, he looked at Ellie with such contemptuous dislike it hurt like a physical blow. 'Quite a haul. The dogs pick this up?'

'On the conveyor belt to the reclaim

carousel. I never had much faith in sniffer dogs. Seems I was wrong.'

The man dropped the packet, glanced with distaste at the magazines, then back to Ellie. 'Why? Why do you do it?' He clamped out the words like gunshots. 'Don't you realise the harm — '

'It's not my bag,' Ellie shouted back at him. 'I haven't done anything.' Her eyes pleaded. This man exuded authority. The two officers were deferential, almost fawning — he must have a high position. Maybe she could convince him she was telling the truth.

'It's not my bag,' she repeated crisply. 'A man calling himself Arthur Smith took my bag at Heathrow Airport. I checked this one in, believing it to be mine. OK, I shouldn't have been so gullible, but that's my only crime. Please — let me sketch the man. Maybe that'll convince you there was someone.'

'Anyone can sketch a face,' the man snapped. 'That doesn't prove a thing.'

'It's the usual story, Rodd.' The

15

officer finally took off his dark glasses and rubbed the bridge of his nose. 'Says she's never used drugs. It's not her bag. Someone must have put it there.'

'Not very original, is it?' The newcomer looked over his head.

'It's true.' Ellie was desperate. Somehow it was vital to convince him she was innocent. 'I've come to Vancouver to do a job — one I really wanted. Why should I jeopardise that? I've never been remotely involved in drugs. I wouldn't ever — ' She broke off and turned pleading eyes on them once more. 'At least let me sketch the man at Heathrow.' Her eyes held the man they called Rodd, trying not to waver in the face of his scorn.

'It's nothing to do with me. I'm here to see some plant samples through customs. I've merely been directed to the wrong room.' His voice was icy.

Ellie swallowed. The loathing, the dislike from all three men was palpable. She didn't know how to deal with the fearful brick wall of enmity. But — she was innocent, and a fighting spirit surged through her.

'It's time I had a lawyer, if you're not prepared to let me defend myself, and identify the man who conned me.'

'After you've been searched, you can make a phone call. We don't have any more time to waste. There's a plane due from Bangkok.' Officer Henderson was at the door.

'Just a minute, Gus.' Rodd detained him. 'Just what does she hope to do?'

'Says she's an artist, and could give us a photo fit of her Mr Smith.'

Rodd leaned against the wall, arms folded, looking down at Ellie. His jaw was tense, and a tiny pulse began to beat in his throat. She sensed an enormous effort of control as his scrutiny intensified.

'You could give it a try.' The words were harshly ground out, and Ellie's head went back.

'Who are you?' She resented his arrogant assumption of control, and his intense disapproval of her.

'This is Rodd Pallister.' Gus Henderson's voice had a touch of reverential awe. 'He's a very important man in Vancouver, especially on the Island.' His tone suggested Ellie was at fault for not knowing that.

Her dislike for Mr Pallister grew. 'I've not had a chance to get acquainted with Vancouver society. I was hoping to start with Bob Burgess.'

'You know Bob Burgess?' Rodd snapped. 'Why were you meeting him?'

'That's none of your business,' she retorted.

'It'll do you no good being rude to Mr Pallister,' Officer Henderson rebuked her, then picked up the phone. 'Julie, can you come in here? Drug search.'

'No!' Ellie gasped in horror.

'Just a second.' Rodd Pallister took the receiver. 'Hold off a moment, Julie. Thanks.' He replaced the receiver.

'As a favour to me, Gus, let her try a sketch. See what she comes up with. It's probably a stall, but what's to lose?

I'll hang on in here while she does it. You meet your next plane. I'll get Julie in if you want to make if official.'

Ellie held her breath. Where Rodd Pallister fitted in she didn't know, but he seemed to have sufficient influence to give orders to the customs officers.

Gus Henderson hesitated for a second, then shrugged. 'If you say so, Rodd. She says she has a drawing pad. No need to send Julie in — '

'I'd prefer it,' Ellie interrupted. She didn't trust these men and she certainly didn't relish being alone with Rodd Pallister.

'We'll be back in half an hour. Unless you come up with something interesting we'll proceed with the search.' Gus Henderson was chillingly formal as he left the room with his young colleague.

A small, dark-haired girl in customs officer uniform came into the room. Her face lit up when she saw Rodd. 'Mr Pallister. Great to see you again. How's the Island? And the family? You in town for long?'

'Hi, Julie. Good to see you, too.' A half-smile played round his lips. It was the first time, after his initial entrance, Ellie had seen his features soften. 'I'm in town for a day or two, before I head back to Dalton.' He paused, and the smile vanished. 'The family's OK,' he added abruptly.

Ellie tried to shut them both out, concentrating on her mental image of the man at Heathrow. Frowning, she recalled now how frequently he'd turned his face away, wiping his eyes with a handkerchief, and blowing his nose. Ugh! Crocodile tears — obviously a good actor — and what a fool she'd been to fall for it. Rapidly, she started to sketch, uneasily aware of the tall man watching her. It didn't take long. After fifteen minutes she sat back, pushing the paper away.

'That's Arthur Smith.'

Julie was still by the door. Rodd Pallister was sitting opposite, still staring sombrely at Ellie. He took the drawing, glanced at the portrait, then sharply back at Ellie. She knew it was a good representation. Portrait likenesses presented no problem to her.

'Arthur Smith' had a pudgy face, soft, almost feminine features, and a receding hairline which showed his main peculiarity — oddly-shaped ears.

Rodd frowned. 'You know this man well?' It was an accusation.

'If course I don't. I've told you, I met him at Heathrow, this morning, before I checked in.'

This morning! It seemed months ago. All her confident excitement at the prospect of her new job had drained away. Her situation was grim. No-one believed her story, and now she'd completed the sketch, she knew it didn't, as Rodd Pallister had said, prove a thing. Just a man at an airport — just a desperate figment of her 'guilty' imagination to the authorities! She felt very lonely. She needed someone on her side.

'I can make a telephone call? I have that right, don't I?' She glanced at her

21

watch, still at British time. In the claustrophobic atmosphere of the inter-view room she'd lost track of the hours. It was 2 a.m. — 6 p.m. British Columbia time. Her parents would be asleep, but it couldn't be helped. Her eyes were gritty with exhaustion, her usually animated face, pale and drawn. Anxiety and reaction were seeping in, as the reality of her plight struck home.

'Who do you want to phone?' Rodd's eyes were glued to the drawing.

'My father, in London.' She dragged out the words reluctantly. She didn't want to talk to this man — he had obviously judged her without trial. She longed for the warmth and affection of her father's voice. He knew she was innocent.

'You can phone when the customs officers come back. What are you doing here — officially?'

'I've told the immigration authorities. If you're nothing to do with them, I don't have to tell you.'

'I could be of help to you.'

It was the first concession he'd made, but Ellie didn't believe him, remaining stubbornly silent. She'd had enough of giving answers which nobody believed. Besides, Rodd Pallister made her nervous.

He got up and began to pace the small room. Julie stepped away from the door to give him more room. He stopped behind Ellie's chair. The hairs of her head pricked with tension. He was so close, she could almost feel the brush of his forearms as he stretched his hands on the back of her chair.

His tone threatened. 'You're in a bad situation, Ellie Jones. London's a long way off. You need friends here.'

'That shouldn't trouble you.' She was defiant. He was the last person she'd expect to help her. His attitude was very clear, and it was a relief when Officers Henderson and Brent returned.

Rodd swung round. 'Any luck?'

They shook their heads. 'Not this time. We didn't expect it — just routine.

What about Miss Jones here?'

Rodd handed over the sketch with a warning look, and a negative nod, but it was too late to stop their reaction.

'I don't believe it — '

'It can't be — it's — '

Rodd cut in. 'Not now. Julie, can you stay here with her?' He nodded towards Ellie. 'I want a private word with Gus. We need to check on something.'

'Please, can't I make a phone call? I've done what I wanted — drawn the man responsible for these.' Ellie gestured at the white packets and the lurid magazines. 'How long are you going to keep me here?'

'As long as it takes,' Rodd Pallister answered, and left the room with the sketch, followed by the two men.

Ellie rubbed her aching eyes. 'Am I allowed to walk about?'

Julie nodded. 'Of course. Would you like coffee, or tea?'

It was the first kind thing Ellie had heard since leaving the plane, and it nearly unnerved her. She nodded

24

silently, and Julie picked up the phone.

Coffee revived her. She even managed to chat to the young officer, who at least seemed prepared to keep an open mind about her. The men had clearly marked her as a hardened criminal of the worst kind.

It seemed an age before they came back, and her spirits nose-dived. They looked grimmer than ever, and she prepared for the worst.

Rodd Pallister still held the drawing, but now he also held several other documents. 'We've been in touch with Heathrow,' he began, never taking his eyes from Ellie. 'They've come up with something really interesting.'

2

Ellie waited to hear what he had to say. She was innocent, she knew that. Let them try to prove her guilty!

Gus Henderson said, 'Your bag's turned up at Heathrow Airport. Caused a full-scale security alert. It was left under a cafeteria table. No identifying tag, but it fits your description. I'll need a check list of the contents, to tally with information we've received.'

'No problem. I know exactly what was in it. After I've done that, can I go?'

'It's not that simple. You could have left the bag there deliberately.'

Ellie sighed. Gus Henderson had made his mind up, and was determined to be as difficult as possible.

Rodd intervened. 'What could help is your sketch of Arthur Smith — alias Daniel Merton — real name Peter Ray. A known drug trafficker.'

Ellie gasped. 'That sad, old man?'

'He's under forty, and a very good actor. The police have never been able to prove anything against him. Now maybe — '

'But where does that leave me? Surely you believe me now.'

'It could all be an elaborate set-up. You and Peter Ray could be partners — ' Henderson started to say.

'For goodness' sake.' Ellie groaned and put her head in her hands. It was hopeless.

'Look,' Tony Brent said stepping forward, 'we'd like to nail this guy. So would the authorities in several countries, including Great Britain. London's drug squad is following it up right now. You'll have to stay here and help us out.'

Ellie jumped up. 'Why should I? You've made this as hard as possible. Now, I can just walk right out of here, and make things hard for you. You've kept me here, denied me a lawyer, threatened to search me — '

'Stop it.' Rodd Pallister's voice cracked across her rising shrillness. 'You're not cleared at all. Don't forget — they have all the evidence they need against you — very good evidence. Calm down and be sensible.'

'Why should I listen to you, Mr Pallister. What's it to do with you?'

His eyes raked over her, completely and slowly, before he quietly answered, 'Because, Miss Ellie Jones, these officers are placing you in my custody.'

Ellie's hands flew to her mouth to stop the yell of protest. Half strangled, it came out as a gasp. 'What do you mean? How can they do that? You can't!'

She swung round to Julie, who was still in the room. 'They can't, can they? Abduct me?'

The girl looked acutely uncomfortable. 'Abduction's a bit strong. I — I don't know. I don't have all the facts but, because you were found carrying drugs, there's a cast-iron case to hold you in custody.'

'But why him? I'd rather spend time in prison.'

'I don't think you would,' Julie murmured. 'It's not exactly what you're used to, I guess.'

'This is outrageous. I demand a lawyer!'

Without a word, Gus Henderson picked up the phone, looked across at Rodd, and dialled a number.

Fifteen minutes later, Ellie was in the depths of despair. She might have known it! The lawyer was, of course, from Vancouver — and a friend of Rodd's. Gus had tersely outlined the case before handing the phone to her. The lawyer, Joe Williams, had listened patiently, been pleasant and reasonable, but had advised her to go along with the authorities.

If they wanted Rodd Pallister to take her into custody, and he was prepared to stand surety, then she should comply, he advised her. He vouched for Rodd as an eminent, respected, and powerful Canadian citizen, with influence in many quarters of British Columbia. She would be lucky to have him as a friend. He said he'd keep in touch and that she was going to need legal representation from the sound of things.

Ellie couldn't understand it. It was a gigantic conspiracy, a ghastly, nightmare web spun tightly around her, with Rodd Pallister the all-powerful spider, and her the already pinioned fly!

'Well?' the spider asked, frowning impatiently.

'Do I really have a choice?'

'No.' It was decisive. 'Come along, I've spent enough time here.' He picked up the big, leather case from the table, seized her arm, nodded to the three customs officials, and took her out of the room.

A silver-grey Mercedes was parked outside the terminal in flagrant disregard of the rules. Of course it was Rodd's, and, of course, no-one seemed to mind. The airport staff all seemed to know him, from the security guards to the baggage attendants outside.

One of them held the car door open for her. 'Hi, Rodd. Nice to see you. How are things on the Island?'

'Fine. Can't wait to get back.' Rodd smiled as he slid into the driver's seat and revved the engine. 'See you.'

It was early evening. Traffic was light. Ellie had an impression of wide streets, ringed by mountains, some snow-capped. Every now and then she glimpsed the waters of the river or harbour.

'Had you fixed a hotel?' Rodd's enquiry was casual.

'Bob Burgess booked me in at the Continental — just for tonight. I'll find — I was going to find my own accommodation after that.' She was deliberately aloof — she couldn't help the situation she was in, but she didn't have to like it.

'I'll give him a call when we get in.'

'I can call him. Being under suspicion doesn't deprive me of the faculties. And just where are we going?'

'My place. Just over the bridge here.' He swung the car in a left turn, down a couple of blocks, and on to a waterfront, fronted by tall apartment buildings.

Rodd Pallister occupied the penthouse of the tallest building. It was the most luxurious apartment Ellie had ever seen, but she was determined to be unimpressed. A grey-haired woman met them in the hall with a welcoming smile.

'Althea, this is Ellie Jones. She'll be staying here — the guest suite,' Rodd emphasised.

Ellie wondered how many girls he brought back who weren't accommodated in the guest room. Antagonistic as she felt towards him, she had to admit he was a most attractive man. She glowered at him. He must have a girlfriend — or be married perhaps?

'I know you're out tonight, Althea. I'll get us something to eat. Don't wait.'

Ellie was alarmed. Was she to be imprisoned here on her own with the tall Canadian? It was all very well for the customs officer, and the lawyer, to vouch for him — she didn't trust their judgement, and she certainly didn't trust him!

'I've left some food in the kitchen — if you're sure you don't need me — '

'I don't — thanks,' Rodd said. 'I'll see you in the morning. Good-night.'

The two of them were left alone. He took her bag and motioned her to follow him. He opened the door of a beautifully-furnished room, large enough to house several guests.

'Bathroom's through there, and the deck has a view over the city.' His cool, grey eyes assessed her.

She suddenly felt grubby, and in need of a shower.

'I'll leave you for a while. Supper in half an hour.'

Ellie sat on the king-size bed and looked around. It was better than the cells, she had to concede.

★   ★   ★

Rodd was in the kitchen. A cork popped as she came in.

'You can phone home if you want.' He nodded towards the wall phone.

'No thanks. I prefer to wait until I'm on my own.' She longed to hear her mother, or her father's voice, but she wasn't going to let him know that. And what was she to tell them — at this stage? Now her initial panic had receded, she was reluctant to worry them.

'Please yourself,' Rodd said with infuriating calm.

'I will.'

'You still don't understand, do you? You're behaving like a stubborn child.'

'There's no need to be rude. This isn't my choice.'

'Nor mine,' he said quietly.

'You set it up. There was no need for you to interfere — '

'You'd prefer the police station, would you?'

'Yes. No. I don't know — I feel — trapped. I hate that.'

34

He took glasses from a cupboard. 'You're tired. It's been a long flight, and you've had no sleep. It's dawn in Britain. Eat something, have a glass of wine, and go to bed. Go through to the deck. There's a fine view of the river and Granville Island. I'll bring the food.'

His concern, genuine or not, weakened her will. She was hungry, and there was a delicious smell from a saucepan — a dish of green noodles steamed on a hot-plate nearby. 'Can I help?' she asked.

He seemed surprised. 'You can take out the bread — and salad.'

She nearly dropped the plates as she stepped out between the huge plate glass doors at the end of the sitting-room. The view was breathtaking — an eagle's eye view over much of the city.

Ellie put the plates on a table already laid for a meal, went to the rail and looked down. Usually she didn't mind heights, but strain, and lack of sleep, made her head spin. Beneath her, nothingness stretched, seemingly for ever, down to the toytown street below. She leaned against the rail, feeling weak and giddy, unable to move back, terrified of over-balancing. The deck floor seemed to rise up, and she staggered and nearly fell . . .

Suddenly, she was grasped firmly round the waist, pinned against Rodd's hard body. She heard his angry shout.

'What on earth are you doing? That's no way out of the mess you're in!'

He pulled her away from the rail, but didn't let go of her. Turning her to face him, he gave her a shake. 'Snap out of it. Nothing's that bad.'

Ellie pulled herself away, sitting weakly on a chair near the table. 'I — I was looking at the view and felt dizzy, that's all.' She clapped her hand to her mouth. 'No! You didn't think . . . ? What did you think I was going to do? Jump off the building?' She couldn't help it — laughter bubbled up from her throat and her shoulders shook.

'I don't see anything funny.' Rodd was sombre.

'But it's all so silly — and — and so melodramatic.' She suddenly felt better, and looked at him curiously. 'You didn't seriously think I'd even contemplate such a thing.'

'It's been known.'

'What — from up here?'

'Not here particularly — but people on drugs — '

'I am not on drugs. Will you get that into your head? They are no part of my life — never have been. What's the matter with you?'

Adrenalin drove the last vestige of dizziness from her. Ellie was furious. She stood up and thrust her face into his. She saw a flicker of something she couldn't identify in his grey eyes. Not fear. Rodd Pallister wasn't a man to show fear even if he felt it, but it was something akin — some intense emotion that defied description — something which scared her even in her anger.

'Why won't you accept what I say? I

thought, maybe after my bag was found at Heathrow, and the drawing — ' A thought occurred to her. 'What if the dogs hadn't found the bag — and I'd gone through customs?'

'No hope of that. The bag would have disappeared — a baggage handler maybe — someone certainly on the look-out for it. They slipped up, leaving your bag at Heathrow.' He put his hands on her shoulders, pressing down on the flesh. The touch scorched through her — her knees weakened, and she fell back on to the chair. His voice was controlled. 'Sit down — and eat. I'll keep an open mind — for now.'

'Big of you,' she muttered, but the intensity of emotion she'd seen in his expression sobered her. There were fires in him which she was wary of releasing, but at the same time, she tingled with nervous excitement.

He poured wine into two large, crystal goblets, and presented Ellie, for the first time, with a smiling, civilised face. He lifted his glass to hers. 'I suggest a cessation of hostilities for the rest of the evening. I should think you've had enough action for one day.'

Ellie responded automatically, raised her own glass, and drank thirstily. The wine tasted of peaches and honeyed butter, warming a relaxing pathway through her body. After one glass, and a plateful of pasta in a delicious sauce, she began to let go. Her head dropped over supper, but she managed to make it to the sofa for coffee. Rodd went out for cream, and that was the last thing she remembered of the evening.

When he came back, Ellie was fast asleep. He shook her gently, called her name, but, exhausted by twenty-four hours without sleep, and the turbulent events at the airport, she could only blink, mumble, and fall asleep again.

Rodd looked down at her for a long time, his face darkly sober, yet, as he bent to pick her up, his grim mouth softened a little as, in her sleep, she flung an arm around his neck, turning into his chest with a soft sigh. With an ironic smile, he carried her into the guest bedroom. His visit to the airport had turned out to be more than he'd bargained for, too.

Next morning, it took Ellie a few moments to recall how she came to be in a king-size bed in such luxurious surroundings. The last thing she remembered was Rodd bringing in the coffee . . . She sat up quickly. How did she come to be wearing the outsize T-shirt, which doubled as a nightie? Surely he wouldn't have dared . . . ?

There was a knock on the door and Althea came in with a tray. 'Breakfast, Ellie? You've slept the clock round.'

'How did I . . . ?'

'Don't worry. I put your nightshirt on. I hope you don't mind. I came back late, and Rodd asked me to look in on you. Your clothes were twisted and you didn't look at all comfortable. I found that in your bag.'

'Thanks. No, I don't mind at all.' Ellie's relief made her hungry. The scrambled eggs and bacon looked good.

Althea set out a table by the window. Hot coffee steamed fragrantly. She drew the curtains back. 'Wonderful day. Spring's really arrived.'

Ellie jumped out of bed and went over to the window. The view was even more dazzlingly impressive in the bright sun.

'I can't wait to go down there.' She tossed back sleep-tousled curls. 'After that yummy-looking breakfast, of course.'

Althea looked embarrassed. 'I'm sorry. Rodd gave me instructions. He had to go out early, but — er — you're not to leave the apartment. Not until he gets back, at least.'

'What! How long's that going to be?'

'I don't know. Some time today, I'm sure.'

'But — you can't mean it. I'm under house arrest?'

'I'm sorry,' Althea repeated. 'There's nothing I can do — really. There are plenty of books, music, videos . . . '

The woman looked so uncomfortable, Ellie put a hand on her arm. 'Don't worry, it's not your fault but, honestly, I'd come back again. I'd just like to go down to the waterfront, but if you say I can't, it's OK.'

The telephone rang and Althea escaped thankfully.

Philosophically, Ellie sat down to breakfast. At least it was deluxe house arrest, she thought, shaking out a snowy napkin and putting it incongruously across her bare knees.

Althea came back, carrying the phone. 'It's for you. Bob Burgess.' She sounded impressed as she handed over the receiver.

'Am I speaking to Ellie Jones?' a voice with a strong accent asked.

'That's right.' Ellie swallowed a mouthful of creamy egg. 'I'm sorry about what happened yesterday. They wouldn't let me meet you.'

'I know. Rodd explained the situation this morning. I'm real sorry, too — for all the — trouble.' He sounded tentative.

'I'd like to meet you as soon as possible,' Ellie said quickly. 'I'm dying to start work — but all my equipment — it's still in London.'

'Ah! Yes, Rodd told me. Well, that's no problem. We can loan you some, but we'll have to wait awhile now.'

'But we can get together, can't we? You can brief me, tell me what I can do, where to go — '

'Well, I'd prefer to wait until this — er — business is clarified. I just phoned to make contact. As soon as Rodd gives me the all clear, I'll give our first meeting top priority.'

Ellie's disappointment rose in her throat, but she was powerless to do anything. Bob Burgess was a busy man, and she'd been lucky to have the contact through Conservation Planet. She didn't know what Rodd had told him, but even a hint of anything illegal, if proven, would be enough to put him off. She bit her lip. That wretched Arthur Smith! It was the last time she'd fall for anyone's sob story.

'That's good of you, Mr Burgess. I can see your position. Believe me, I want this cleared up as fast as possible.' There was a pause. She rushed on. 'I am innocent you know. I've done nothing illegal.'

'I'm sure things will turn out for the best. Just a misunderstanding, no doubt, but the Customs and Excise people can't be too careful. Don't you agree? I'll wait to hear from Rodd then.'

'Thanks for calling, Mr Burgess.'

Ellie put the phone down, controlling her anger at the way Rodd had pinned her down and taken charge of her life. Also, rested, refreshed, and thinking more clearly than yesterday, she wondered just why he was doing it. It would have been much easier for him simply to let the police take charge. She was sure he wasn't acting on humanitarian grounds to save her the discomfort of a night or so in the cells. She frowned as she chewed the last bit of bacon.

Inaction drove her mad! She'd

breakfasted, explored the apartment, worked out some great theoretical camera shots from the outer deck, read the paper, chatted to Althea, and it was still only early afternoon. The housekeeper was cagey, and evaded all questions about Rodd, except to reiterate what Ellie already knew. Rodd Pallister was very wealthy and very well respected. He was also a leading logging entrepreneur on Vancouver Island. Ellie filed away that nugget of information — it could come in very useful.

The penthouse was large, but by early evening, Ellie found herself pacing restlessly through the rooms.

She left the television running, crept quietly past the kitchen where Althea was working, and cautiously tried the front door. The inner door opened. The outer door to the vestibule and elevators was locked — from the inside! As Ellie turned away, the intercom security buzzer sounded. Althea answered from the kitchen.

Ellie held her breath. If it was a legitimate caller downstairs, Althea might release the door latch from the kitchen. She waited, heard an electronic whirring and, after a few seconds, tried the latch. It opened. She was free!

The apartment building was practically on the dock. A few yards away there was a jetty with moorings. The tiny aquabus she'd seen from the penthouse deck now chugged, large-as-life, to the steps. Enthralled, Ellie ran down the wooden planking and jumped aboard. Whiling away the hours, she'd watched it through Rodd's powerful telescope, and vowed to harbour-hop when she was free. It was a short trip to the other side and back. She had dollars in her pocket and took one out.

Quietly, the girl conductor/driver was eased aside, and a strong hand took Ellie's proffered dollar.

'Put it away, Ellie. You're not going anywhere. Tracey, please turn the bus around — back to the jetty.' An arm clamped her to his side, daring her to struggle. To the gaping handful of passengers, Rodd said, with an easy smile, 'Sorry. Just a little misunderstanding. My girlfriend's caught the wrong bus.'

The small boat turned and crossed the few yards back to the jetty. Parked at the other end, square across the planking, menacing as a Mafia limousine, was the silver-grey Mercedes.

3

Rodd's grip was tight on her waist. 'Into the car please, young lady. I'll speak to you there.'

Ellie struggled. 'Let me go. I'm not your prisoner, and I'm certainly not your girlfriend.'

'Poetic licence. Where were you going on the aquabus?'

'I don't have to tell you, but if you must know, I was sick of being cooped up all day. I slipped out. It wasn't Althea's fault — and I can walk back on my own.'

He didn't release his hold on her until he'd opened the passenger door of the Mercedes and eased her on to the seat. 'Sorry, but I don't trust you. We'll take the elevator from the underground carpark. There's a good reason why you shouldn't be allowed to roam around the city.'

'For goodness' sake — what now?' Ellie muttered, as the car slid down a steep ramp underneath the apartment block.

'I'll tell you when we're upstairs. You'd better apologise to Althea, too.'

'I told you, I'm not a prisoner — nor a child, so please don't treat me like one.'

Rodd stopped the car in a parking place, undid his seat-belt, and turned to face her. He laid his left arm along the back of her seat, grey eyes cloud soft, serious, but more friendly than on the previous day.

'Listen Ellie, this is serious. You've tumbled into something pretty sizeable. You're in enough trouble without treating me as the enemy. I know yesterday wasn't very pleasant for you, but the customs officers were only doing their job, and they do have a particular dislike of drug trafficking, or dealing.' He put his finger to her lips to silence her outraged protest. 'Yes, I know — you're innocent.' He took his hand away from her mouth and looked down at his watch. 'Look, I'm expecting a phone call from the airport. We'll go up to the apartment and talk there. You've got to learn to trust me. If the call confirms what we think, I'd say you need a friend or two in Vancouver!'

Alarm and mutiny, in equal parts, ran through Ellie's head as she and Rodd rode up the elevator. She tried to fathom his expression, but the grey eyes were giving nothing away — yet.

Althea had coffee ready, and said to Ellie, 'Rodd phoned after you went out. I told him you couldn't be far away — he was already on his way back here.'

'I'm sorry, Althea.' Ellie was apologetic. 'I just needed to get out for a while.'

'Very understandable.' The older woman's smile forgave her. 'I'm just so pleased to see you safely back and in Rodd's charge.'

Ellie didn't like the sound of that — nor of Rodd's next question to his housekeeper.

'Have the police phoned?'

'No. No-one today, apart from Mr Burgess.'

'Thanks, Althea. I'll pour coffee. I need to talk to Ellie.'

'Explain would be better,' Ellie burst out, as Althea left. 'Especially your involvement in all this. What exactly is it you do for a living — and what were the police phoning about?'

Rodd sipped his coffee. 'Your 'Arthur Smith' has been found and arrested in London. I'm waiting for the Royal Canadian Police to confirm. They'll probably be around very shortly to interview you.'

'Me! Why me?'

'Isn't it obvious? You're the chief witness — if he's to be successfully convicted.'

'Oh, no.' Ellie put her head in her hands and groaned. How stupid she must seem. She'd been wholly concerned with her own position, simply wanting to be free, and to get on with the job she'd come to Canada to do. Of course, there must be wider implications. 'But that'll be in London. I don't have to go back now, do I?'

'I'm not sure yet. If he's charged, he won't come to trial for a while. They're holding him at present on your word, and portrait sketch, but you'll have to give a statement.'

'I don't understand. Are you a policeman?'

Rodd laughed. 'No. I've too many other things to do!'

'So why are you involved in this?'

The laughter died from his eyes. 'I have a personal interest.'

He answered so bleakly she was loath to ask any more. She took refuge in practicalities. 'What about my work for Conservation Planet? I've only got a limited time here. I should contact them.'

'We can take care of all that after you've seen the police. What do you have to do exactly?'

'Conservation Planet is — '

'Yes, I know all about them.' He was

grim. 'They've got a finger in every environmental pie in the world.'

'They do a lot of good.' Ellie was defensive. 'They help preserve wild-life habitats, monitor pollution . . . I'm to take photographs of the old-forests — look at the problems of the logging industry here. The wild life, too. Bob Burgess has promised to introduce me to the owner of the biggest saw-mills in British Columbia — it's on Dalton Island.'

A door bell chimed, and Rodd jumped to his feet. The look he gave her was mockingly ironic. 'Just goes to show what a small world we live in, Miss Jones. The man Bob Burgess was to introduce you to already has the pleasure of your acquaintance. It's time we were formally introduced.' He held out his hand. 'I own most of the timber on Dalton Island — and a bit more besides. Your Conservation Planet people have sent you right into the thick of it. So you see, Ellie, we were bound to meet. The drugs incident simply pre-empted it.'

He still held her hand, while his lips continued their mocking curve. 'A strange quirk of fate, wouldn't you say? Now, please excuse me. It seems that the police have arrived. Whatever you do, don't go away . . . '

In contrast to the customs officers, the two police officers, in plain clothes, were charm personified. They were accompanied by Joe Williams, the lawyer she'd spoken to from Vancouver Airport. Their deferential manner did much for Ellie's bruised spirit. They treated her as an ally — not an enemy!

They spent an hour checking over her story, going over the facts she'd given to the custom's officials. Finally, they were satisfied, and she signed her statement.

'That's all clear. You've been a great help.' The younger officer, a powerful looking man, was in charge. Tanned, with very blue eyes, he gave Ellie all of his attention.

'I'm glad that's over,' she said, with

relief, as they put away tape recorder and papers. 'Now, I'm free to go.'

Rodd had remained in a corner of the room throughout the questioning, and had appeared to be absorbed in a mass of papers. Ellie had wondered why he'd even bothered to stay. Now he looked up sharply, and the four men exchanged glances.

'Not quite.' Joe Williams avoided her eye. 'The police will want to know what your future plans are.'

'More than that, Mr Williams,' the young officer interjected. 'We'd like to be part of them.' He turned to Ellie. 'Your security is our problem, or rather, our joint problem with London. They and we have the same aim — to convict 'Arthur Smith' and, hopefully, some of his top-level associates. Your evidence will be vital.' He paused.

'But you have it,' Ellie prompted.

'We do — and you'll be appearing in court at the trial. I'm sorry, that's inevitable. But — ' He stopped again, plainly embarrassed, then rushed on.

'This may sound somewhat melodramatic, Miss Jones, but, well, while he remains on remand — and he may even be able to swing bail — you are at risk.'

'What do you mean — at risk?'

Rodd put down the papers and came to sit by her. 'Your Arthur Smith, is a small link in a big chain — a drugs chain which circles half the world. Any information the police can obtain could help to break that chain, but it's a long, grinding, disheartening slog because so many of the villains elude the law, frequently by witness intimidation. Arthur Smith, of course couldn't possibly know you could give such an accurate description — but he and his associates will know now, and what the police fear is, that if you go back to London, which the drug traffickers will expect you to do, you'll be threatened, certainly verbally, perhaps even physically. Do you have family in London?'

'Yes, my parents and Christopher, my brother . . . ' Her green eyes widened. 'They wouldn't, they couldn't — he's only a child! I don't believe it.'

Rodd took her hand. 'Don't be scared. It's simply that we have to tell you what you're up against. There could be millions of dollars in this rotten game, and if we can catch — ' His hand gripped her fingers so painfully that she bit her lip to keep back the cry of pain.

Her own apprehension faded before the rage in his face. 'How do you know all this?' she asked quietly.

He let go her hand, his expression neutralised. 'Common knowledge — and personal involvement.'

'What can I do?' She was trapped, helpless, catching fear from his intensity.

Joe Williams leaned forward. 'There is a way to minimise the risk, if you're prepared to do it. It'll at least keep your family safe — unless — do you live with your parents?'

'No. I've just bought a flat in Camden, quite near them.'

'Forgive me asking. Do you live

alone? A friend shares perhaps?'

'No,' she said. 'I live alone. Why? Is it relevant?'

'It's fortunate that no-one else is living there. By now someone will almost certainly have visited your flat — seeking a pressure point to exert on you.'

'It's unbelievable! My poor flat!' Ellie's fertile imagination called up a horrendous scene of vandalism.

'Don't worry. Nothing will have been harmed. They'll just do a preliminary survey. Arthur Smith would definitely have noted your address on your luggage tag when he switched bags. It's an automatic precaution with villains like him. But they won't know your parents' address and, luckily for us, your surname is fairly common! We've done a lot of telephone-book work!'

'So I can't go back to my own flat at home?'

'Exactly.' The police officer looked relieved.

'I'll go to my parents' then?'

'No — we — Mr Williams, and Rodd, all think it best if you stay here in Canada. Once Arthur Smith's been tried, the danger will ease. You'll have to go back for the trial, of course.'

'When will that be?' Ellie feared she knew the answer.

'Could be a while. Three months at the best. I don't know how speedy your legal processes are.'

'Three months! I can't stay here for three months. I've work to do, a living to earn. Where would I live?'

Rodd looked down at her small hand, still trapped in his. 'You can stay on one of the islands — as my guest. Conservation Planet has extended your assignment. I've been in touch with them, and they're sending a set of requirements which could keep you busy for the next three years, let alone three months!'

Ellie snatched her hand away, although it had been comforting to feel Rodd's strength. 'I wish you'd stop interfering in my life, ordering me about — '

'No-one's ordering you, Miss Jones,' the young police officer placated. 'We just hope you'll help us, that's all. You're under no obligation, but we feel responsible for your safety, and Rodd — well, he owns two of the prettiest islands in the area. You'd surely have a good time there, and you'd be working, too. It would be excellent cover from snoopers.'

Ellie stared at him, flabbergasted. 'He owns two islands here?'

Rodd frowned. 'There are lots of islands. Mine are smallish, but Dalton, the larger one, that's where there's logging at present. Good material for your assignment. And that is where you were going — eventually.'

'But on my terms! I refuse. Absolutely.' It was inconceivable that she should spend an indefinite period of time with the dominant Canadian. 'There's no question of my remaining under his jurisdiction. I'm legally free to go, aren't I?' She appealed to Joe Williams.

His hesitation was only fractional, but the glance he exchanged with Rodd told Ellie it was very important for them to detain her. 'Well — technically, the police could still hold you on suspicion. The drugs were found on you — '

The second officer said hesitantly, 'Ma'am, there's also Mr Bob Burgess. We've spoken to him. He really would prefer you to work with Rodd. Mr Burgess is pretty influential, but he hates adverse publicity. Maybe it's indiscreet to mention this, but he's had plenty lately, what with the logging disputes, and the problems on the island — '

'That doesn't concern us here,' Rodd interjected quickly. Too quickly, Ellie thought.

She felt her professional curiosity stir. Photo journalism was always a challenge. There was something going on here. She needed thinking time.

'You're saying, basically, that Bob Burgess won't help me with my assignment unless I co-operate?'

'I didn't say that,' the officer said gently.

'Why don't we give her a little time to think it over? She's had quite a time since yesterday. Maybe we can have dinner, Ellie. In town, if you'd prefer it, show you the city. It'd be a shame to go back to London without some sightseeing.' Rodd's tone was persuasive.

'I can only remain in Canada if I stay with you. That's it, isn't it?'

'The English police would want to question you, of course, but they're happy to work with us, from here in Vancouver.' Joe Williams snapped shut his case. 'I think Rodd's right. Ellie should have some thinking space. Until tomorrow morning?'

'Again, it looks as though I've no option,' she countered.

No-one spoke, and Ellie knew that was the case.

The police officers and lawyer left, and in the pool of silence that followed, Rodd threw down his challenge.

'Ellie, give it a chance. Forget your outraged sense of hurt, and what you consider unjust treatment. Let's start again — pretend that we've just met and I've invited you out to dinner because I wanted to — ' He gave her a look which made her feel distinctively uneasy.

She hesitated, sure that he was hiding something.

'Shall I take that hesitation as consent?' he asked, smiling. 'I'll give you thirty minutes to get ready.'

4

It took Ellie less than half an hour to shower, wash her hair, and present herself in the only possible going-out clothes she'd packed. The swirling, navy, silk skirt and cream top brought a flicker of admiration to Rodd's eyes, but his comment was a politely distant — 'very suitable.' She was perversely disappointed.

Throughout most of the evening, he maintained that distance, and played the host/guide rôle to perfection. He took her to an elegant restaurant in Canada Place, overlooking the water, and pointed out sights and landmarks as though his one mission in life was to impress her with the beauty of Vancouver. He was courteous, urbane, and a very attractive companion, but Ellie felt he was deliberately maintaining a wall of reserve between them. He asked polite, safe questions about her home and family.

It turned out that he knew London well, and had lived quite close to her parents' home in Hampstead for a few years when he was a young boy. His father had had a short spell in the Canadian Embassy, and had taken his young family on his tour of duty.

'We maybe walked the same streets.' They were at the coffee stage of dinner. The wine had had a mellowing effect, and Rodd was prepared to drop his guard a fraction. 'There was a Sunday market in the square near our house. Did you ever go there?'

Ellie remembered, with pleasure, the family outings there, to browse among the stalls, watch the street entertainers, and drink coffee and eat doughnuts.

'We went there fairly often. I remember it very well.'

'There was a painting of the square by a local artist. My mother persuaded Dad to buy it — a picture of sunlight, lots of people. Perhaps you and your family are in that painting.'

'Do you still have it?' Ellie asked eagerly.

'Of course. It's on the wall at home.'

'Your parents' home?'

'My mother and father are both dead.'

'I'm so sorry. That's — ' Ellie's voice faltered. Rodd's frown discouraged further enquiry. The chink in the wall was closed.

The short silence was broken by a noisy party coming into the restaurant. The discreet alcove table Rodd had requested didn't ensure anonymity. With a whoop of glee, an extremely pretty girl detached herself from the crowd and rushed over, flung her arms around Rodd, and kissed him full on the mouth.

'Rodd Pallister! Where've you been hiding all these weeks? No-one's seen or heard of you for ages. You've been skulking in the backwoods again, you mean thing. We need you to cheer up the social scene. You mustn't mope.

And who's this?' Her bright-eyed smile was full of curiosity as she turned to Ellie.

'Clarrie.' Rodd fended her off with a laugh, but Ellie saw the tension in his jaw, the irritation in his eyes. 'Good to see you, but I'm busy right now. Go back to your party. I don't want the rest of them here.'

Clarrie pouted. 'Why not? You used to love us all — the best party-giver in the area before — ' She stopped abruptly, putting her hand to her mouth, the animation dying from her eyes. 'Oh, Rodd, I'm sorry. Forgive me. We've had a few drinks at the Yacht Club — I never thought — '

'It's all right. Forget it. Just head the rest of them off. We're about to leave anyway.' He signalled the waiter. 'I'll see you sometime, Clarrie. I promise.' Then, as an afterthought, 'This is a business colleague — from England.'

The young girl, chastened, distress on her face, backed away, with a brief nod for Ellie.

Don't I even have a name, Ellie thought, as Rodd bustled her out of the restaurant, using a side door, quickly indicated by the head waiter.

'Sorry about the intrusion, Mr Pallister. I thought you'd be private in that corner.'

'No problem! Excellent meal and service. Thanks.'

Like magic, valet parking produced the Mercedes by the side entrance. Rodd glanced around. The street was quiet, but he was still tense. 'OK, let's go.' The limousine shot away before Ellie had time to fasten her seat-belt!

'Maybe that was the wrong place to take you.' Rodd's hands were taut on the wheel. 'Too public by far.'

'Why all the melodrama? Who was Clarrie, and why are you scared of being seen?'

'I'm not scared, but have you forgotten your position? You're supposed to be in hiding.'

'Oh, come on, Rodd! Who on earth . . . ?'

'You don't know these people,' he snapped. 'You are incredibly naïve.'

'And you do, I suppose,' she retorted sulkily.

'Yes, I do,' he said sombrely.

Ellie was silent. The evening had taken an odd turn. The girl — Clarrie — had upset him. There was more to it than just the possibility of anyone spotting Ellie. She didn't really believe anyone would be out looking for her. It was ludicrous to imagine herself caught up in a criminal situation. Maybe she was naïve, but nothing in her young life, so far, had remotely touched any kind of villainy.

Tentatively, she put out a hand and touched Rodd's arm.

'It's been a lovely evening. Thanks. I don't feel like a prisoner any more.'

He glanced at her. 'You should — because you are!' But his expression suddenly changed, and he spun the car in a sharp left turn. 'OK, Ellie Jones, let's forget that interruption. The night's still young, and I know a place where no-one will possibly recognise us. It should make you feel at home, too.'

His mercurial change of mood startled Ellie, but so much had happened since she'd arrived in Canada that she found herself just accepting it.

Compared with the elegance of Canada Place, the parking lot where Rodd left the Mercedes was distinctly sleazy.

'Is it safe to leave it there?' It was dusk, almost dark, but Ellie could see the flash of white teeth as Rodd smiled at her.

'Safe as anywhere. We'll risk it. We're in the suburbs now.' He held out his hand. 'The Oxford Arms — as near an English pub as you'll find.'

It was dark, noisy, full of young people and, for once, no-one knew Rodd. They were anonymous and, for the next hour, Ellie gave herself up to the rhythm of a live band, finding sensuous pleasure in the perfect attunement of her body with Rodd's as they moved to the tempo of the music. They couldn't talk — it was too noisy to hear a word, and there was no need. The brief interlude was an escape from the pressures of her situation, and she was sorry when Rodd pointed to his watch and mouthed that it was time to go.

'That was fun. Did we have to leave so early?'

'It's well past midnight, and yes, we did. Early start tomorrow — a busy day.'

Ellie frowned. She'd forgotten about the next day, and wondered where on earth she'd find herself the next night. As they arrived back at the penthouse, resentment began to grow again.

Althea had left coffee on a tray. Rodd threw off his jacket, and poured himself a cup. 'I'm going into the study to work for a while. If you'd like to take your drink to bed . . . ' he said pointedly.

Ellie returned to earth with a bump. She felt restless, dissatisfied. He was ushering her off to bed like a child. She glared at him. 'I'm not sleepy.'

Her sharp tone made him turn back.

He blinked at her defiant stare, then slowly put down his cup and jacket.

She backed away, divining his purpose. Her heart began to beat wildly, her mouth was dry. 'Er — all right. I'll just — ' But it was too late.

He moved swiftly, took her in his arms, and kissed her. It was the strangest kiss. It was a dismissive, good-night kiss, not a lover's kiss. It asserted power, dominance, and control; not unfriendly, not erotic either, but the effect was softly sensational to her nerve-endings.

He lifted his head, his mouth soft, relaxed. 'Now — will you go to bed?' His cool, grey eyes dared her to challenge him.

★ ★ ★

Ellie leaned over the deck rail. It was early. The sun had barely risen, yet the city, far below, was stirring with life.

'Not thinking of jumping this time? Have coffee first.'

She spun round. Rodd carried out a tray with juice and coffee.

'I wasn't before. It's not my style at all.'

Rodd nodded approvingly. 'Good girl.'

Ellie bit back her retort, hating the patronising 'good girl,' but Rodd's smile was affable. She wondered for a second whether she'd dreamed that strange kiss. This morning Rodd's manner was brisk and businesslike.

'Meeting with Bob Burgess for breakfast at nine — on the dock. Then to Vancouver Island. I need to stay overnight, then, tomorrow, I'll take you to Dalton Island. That's where you'll be staying — and working.'

'Can't I go straight to Dalton?' She wondered if she could face another night imprisoned with Rodd.

'It's not convenient. I hope you don't mind.'

She shrugged. 'Do I have a choice?'

'No, I'm afraid not. I think you might enjoy Timberlands.'

'Timberlands?'

'The Pallister family home — north of Victoria. We should leave now. You're packed?'

She nodded. At least she would soon be working, doing what she loved to do. If only she had her own equipment, but that was probably in police custody, too, only thousands of miles away.

'You're not in police custody, Ellie.'

She jumped. Had she spoken out loud? How else . . . ?

'Your face gives you away like crazy.'

He put out a hand and rumpled her hair. 'You're very transparent. You don't fit the stereotype at all.'

'What stereotype?' she snapped.

'British reserve. Cold!' He held her stare for a moment. 'Come on, let's go and see what Bob Burgess has to offer.'

The Mercedes, chauffeur-driven this time, took them to a docking wharf a few hundred yards from Canada Place. Ellie was puzzled. She'd assumed they'd travel to Vancouver Island by ferry.

'Takes too long.' Rodd's reply to her question was laconic. 'And it's too public. Here's Bob.'

A tubby, cheerful-looking man came out of a nearby coffee diner, hands outstretched to Ellie.

'Miss Jones — at last! What a time you're having. Most unexpected. I hope Rodd's been taking good care of you. Sorry about the airport — er — mix-up, but the police advised me to leave — not to meet you. All very unfortunate.'

He pumped both her arms up and down, then clapped Rodd on the back.

'Breakfast's on the stove — Mo's back room. Private, like you said.' He held up his hand. 'No — I don't want to know the ins and outs. Best if we just stick to the job in hand. Miss Jones' — Ellie's — work on the islands. I've got all your replacement photographic gear, and a bit more besides.'

'That's great. Can I see it?'

'Surely. After breakfast.'

Breakfast took longer than she'd

expected. It was man-sized, and she found it hard to cope with even half of it. Bob and Rodd obligingly shared her leftovers.

'Lumberjack appetites. That's what we both are basically.' Bob laughed at her wide-eyed surprise, as he mopped up the remains of his eggs, bacon, grits and hash-browns. 'More coffee, then down to business.'

Ellie declined the coffee. She was anxious to get down to business.

Bob Burgess, as a government forestry executive, was familiar with all the forestry lands in British Columbia, and controlled all their timber cutting rates. A powerful and influential man, he could make or break Ellie's success.

She was curious about his motives. 'Can I ask why you've allowed me to photograph the logging operations? So many pressure groups are against cutting down the trees — it's an explosive issue here, isn't it?'

'That's so, and I make no bones. I'm against these nuisance groups who are trying to stop us cutting the timber. We need the timber for all manner of things, and the area needs the jobs.'

Ellie realised she had to step warily. 'But the forests, aren't they being denuded — won't they be lost to posterity?'

'I see someone's been getting to you, Ellie. We don't denude — we harvest and control! I've let you in here, so you can make a fair and objective case. I like the idea of it in pictures, too, but if I find you teaming up with these tree-spiking lunatics — ' He frowned. 'Rodd, have you been talking to her?'

'Now, Bob, as if I would. You know my views — down the middle. A lot of my land is old growth, and stays as it is.'

'Lucky you can afford it,' Bob grumbled.

'I promise I'll be totally objective,' Ellie interjected. She didn't relish an argument at that moment. She simply wanted to get on and take some pictures.

'Equipment's over there in that box — and don't forget, I get to see all your material before it goes to Conservation Planet.'

'Naturally.' She was already diving into the box. 'Fantastic,' she cried, a few minutes later. 'It's much more up-to-date than mine. And these lenses are great. How did you — '

'All Rodd's doing. He gave me a list of what was in your bag at Heathrow, and added a few bits, too, I suspect.'

'Thanks — both of you. I'll take good care of it.' She stroked the camera, the very latest model. Her fingers itched to focus.

A young man put his head round the door. 'The plane is ready when you are, Mr Pallister.'

'Plane?'

'I told you — faster, more private. Bob, you won't forget Ellie's officially left Canada, if anyone should ask — and you'll let me know, of course, if there are any enquiries about her.'

'Understood. We'll be in touch. Best

of luck, Ellie . . . '

Rodd took his eyes from the controls to watch Ellie, camera glued to her eyes, clicking every few seconds. 'You'll run out of film before you start. Put that down and just use your eyes,' he commanded. 'I'll fly you over the islands for you to photograph them again if you like.'

'Please. It's stunning.'

After take-off, Rodd had circled the harbour in his sea-plane to give her a birds'-eye view of Vancouver, before heading down the Strait of Georgia, towards Victoria, on the southernmost point of Vancouver Island. Other islands, small and not-so-small, spread beneath them in the glittering blue water. He flew the plane low enough for Ellie to see the picturesque village, tiny marinas, forests and bays. It was an ever-changing panorama, and she was enchanted.

Rodd pointed down. 'A pod of whales — Orcas — over there. Try the camera, and use the water filter.'

But this time she used her eyes to watch and enjoy the huge black beasts throwing up their ocean spouts. Hadn't Rodd promised to fly her again?

The next time he pointed down, they were almost on to Vancouver Island. She saw a small beach, cut in a thick, forested inlet, and a wooden building glimpsed through the trees. Rodd dropped the sea-plane in a gradual descent. As they hit the water, spray flung against the windows, the engine cut to a throb, and the plane bobbed along on its floats towards a wooden platform at the end of a jetty.

Ellie saw a figure standing on the platform. It was a woman in cut-off jeans and a cotton T-shirt. Her very long, red hair, sun hat and glasses totally obscured her face, but as the plane came close she raised her arm in greeting.

'Rodd!' A sweet, thin voice floated out to meet them.

Rodd punched open the window flap, leaned out, and waved back.

'Donna, I'm back.'

The girl jumped up and down in excitement, then suddenly stopped, shaded her eyes with both hands and took an uncertain step forward. The sea-plane was almost at the platform, when she turned and ran very fast, back up the jetty, to disappear into the thick trees.

'Damn. She's seen you.' Rodd's smile had vanished, too. He revved the engine as though to urge the fragile plane faster.

'You didn't say I was to act invisible here.' Ellie knew she sounded childish, but she couldn't help her disappointment. The excitement of the trip drained away. What an odd woman — girlfriend, or wife? 'Who . . . ?' she started to ask, but before the plane had come to rest, Rodd was out of the door.

Surefootedly, he swung along the floats, secured the plane and opened the passenger door. 'Can you manage? I must go after Donna. There's a path, through the trees, leading up to the house. Ted'll be there. Leave your bag in the plane — someone'll fetch it for you.'

And he was gone, sprinting along the beach.

Ellie hauled her case from the back of the plane. She'd feel safer if her bags were with her — not sure about Ted, nor about wandering into a strange house on her own.

Slowly, she made her way towards the path Rodd had indicated. It turned out to be a wide drive, obviously used by four-wheeled vehicles, and much longer than she'd imagined. It stretched away through the forest, and she could see no end.

Massive trees soared above her, blocking out the sky. It was like no woodland she'd been in before. She wanted to explore, but hesitated to stray from the path. It was like being in the heart of a primeval forest, then, quite abruptly, the path led out on to a shingled beach, twisted at a sharp right angle, and there was Timberlands.

A white-haired man came down the steps of a wooden veranda. 'You must be Ellie Jones. Welcome. Rodd phoned to expect you both. Where is he?'

'Hello — er — he ran off to find a girl who — ran off. I think — because she saw me — I think,' she repeated, aware it sounded pretty confused.

'That'll be Donna.' He shook his head and tutted. 'No call for Rodd to run off and leave a guest. Bad manners. Let me make amends. How about a drink? Lunch is ready, but it's cold, so it'll keep.'

Ellie rarely drank at lunchtime, but it seemed a time for breaking the rules again, so she nodded. 'Please. Can I help?'

'No. You sit down. Admire the view. Won't be a sec.'

She lay back on a lounger, and did as she was told. Timberlands was single-storey, spreading extensively and opulently along the shore-line. The view was lovely, and she could see the islands were going to give her scenic indigestion. She'd have to ration their effect.

With a chinking of glass, the old man returned with an ice bucket, crystal flutes and champagne!

'Goodness!' was all Ellie could say.

The man chuckled. 'Best way I know of making amends for bad manners. I'm Ted Pallister, Rodd's uncle. I'm the sort of resident housekeeper of Timberlands. Finally pensioned off — by that boy, would you believe?'

By the time 'that boy' joined them, Ellie and Uncle Ted were the best of friends. Ted was a natural charmer, and wore his eighty years lightly. Well into her second glass of champagne, Ellie realised she had told him all about herself.

Ted talked about the islands with love and enthusiasm. He'd travelled the world, but always returned thankfully to the islands.

'It's a wonderful life here, Ellie. Quite different from the mainland. You'll love it, and once you start to explore the other islands, you'll never want to leave.'

'Did you always live here at Timberlands?' Ellie asked.

'No. I had a place down the coast. My brother, Jonathon — that's Rodd's father — and I bought up a whole load of land around here after the war. I stayed to log the forests, to fish and have a good time. Jon was a diplomat, but he kept coming back. He and Harriet loved the place.'

'They died — Rodd said.'

The old man momentarily looked his age. He drained his glass. 'Yes, Jon and Harriet didn't live to enjoy their last years here. A tragedy. Rodd didn't tell you what happened?'

She shook her head. 'No, just that they were dead.'

'He'll tell you, in his own good time — if he wants to. He's still mighty sensitive about it. And here he is — at last. Where've you been, boy?'

'Hi, Ted. Sorry. I'd no idea I'd be so long.'

'Did you find Donna? Ellie tells me she dashed away before you landed.'

'No. She's still holed up in the forest. She'll come back for supper.' Rodd turned to Ellie. 'Sorry I left you like that, but I can see you've been in good hands.'

'I've enjoyed talking to your uncle.'

Ted got to his feet. 'Lunch now, and then I need to talk business with you, Rodd. I'll show Ellie to her room first. How long's she staying here?'

'Only overnight — ' He hesitated before adding, 'Then I'm taking her to Dalton Island. That'll be her base.'

Ted had picked up Ellie's suitcase, but dropped it in his surprise. 'Dalton Island? Is that wise? Especially just now. I had a call from Pete yesterday. He's worried about the latest arrivals. All these so-called tree preservers. Just a load of hippies, I call them, wanting a free holiday. They could mean trouble.'

'Uncle Ted — most of them are committed conservationists. Misguided or not, some of them do believe we're destroying the forests. They have a point of view, and they're entitled to express it.'

'Well, I wish they wouldn't express it on our land. I'm surprised at you, Rodd. They can cause a heck of a lot of damage. Trouble is, you never know what they're going to get up to next — or where.' He looked at Ellie and clapped his hand to his forehead. 'Ah, I see it now. Ellie's told me what she's going to do. Perfect cover. She's to find out what goes on, and report back to you. Clever move, Rodd — bit devious though. Not your usual style.'

'Ted!' Rodd's voice whiplashed across the deck. 'That's not the idea at all.'

But Ted had made up his mind. 'Of course not. Come along, Ellie.'

He chuckled to himself as he went into the house, but Ellie remained, staring at Rodd. All the talk about her own safety was hogwash. Rodd Pallister was using her for his own purposes — to find out what the tree saboteurs were up to. If he'd been straight with her, she might not have objected, but he'd conned her all along with his ridiculous melodrama about drug gangs.

Turning on her heel, she followed Ted, ignoring Rodd's, 'Ellie, wait a minute.' She wasn't going to play his game!

5

Uncle Ted showed Ellie to a guest suite which was twice as large, and twice as luxurious, as Rodd's Vancouver guest room.

Ted Pallister, quite unaware of the tension he'd caused, left her with a cheery smile. 'Plenty of time to freshen up. We'll eat when you're ready. Just follow your nose to the dining-room.'

Ten minutes later, Ellie stepped into a long corridor with several doors, all closed, stretching the length of the house. It was very quiet, and she wondered how many other people lived at Timberlands.

As Ted had indicated, the route to the dining-room was unmistakeable. A wonderful, savoury aroma wafted her towards a large room where lunch was set for four. Rodd and Ted, absorbed in conversation, broke off immediately they saw her. She guessed, from the look on Ted's face, that he was in trouble! Well, she was grateful to him that he'd given the game away. At least she was forewarned, but there was no reason not to enjoy the delicious lunch.

'Nectar — trawled from the islands' sea beds,' Ted said, ladling out a bowlful of soup for her, 'though Anna calls it fish chowder.'

'Anna?' Ellie picked up her spoon. Not another tree flitting waif?

'Anna and Buck Simpson, they help me run this place. They'll be back tomorrow. They're on the mainland today.'

'They should go separately,' Rodd said. 'I've told you, Ted — until Donna's better. It's too much for you on your own. You see what happened today.'

'Rubbish. I'm not in my dotage yet. She's just too cunning for all of us, and, you've got to accept it, she's not going to — '

'More soup, Ellie?' Rodd interrupted hastily.

Ellie bent her head, missing the meaningful glance between the two men, but they understood each other well. After a short silence, they turned on the Pallister charm and set out to entertain her with more tales of the islands.

Over coffee, the conversation slowed to a trickle. Rodd looked more and more preoccupied, and Ted began to yawn. 'All that champagne,' he apologised. 'I'll rest this afternoon, Rodd. What about our guest here?'

'I have to go out.' Rodd was abrupt.

Ellie sensed his relief that the meal was over, and she guessed he wanted to resume his search for Donna. She put in quickly, 'I have plenty to do. I did a lot of research in London on British Columbia, and there are tapes and notes I need to go over — '

'And there's some stuff from Conservation Planet you haven't had yet. It's in the plane. I'll get it for you.'

'Please don't worry about me. After all, I'm here to work,' Ellie put in.

'I think we could all do with a little time to ourselves this afternoon. We'll meet again for a drink before supper. Will that suit you, Ellie?'

She nodded before going to her room. 'Whatever you say, Rodd.'

Ellie fully intended to work, to revise the background to the main issue on the gulf islands — the logging disputes. The breathtaking beauty of the area had already won her heart. She partially undressed, put on a cotton robe, settled herself on the huge, embracing bed, and began to read the local newspapers she'd bought.

The pace is hotting up in the dispute over whether logging in British Columbia should be halted, or at least curtailed, by government legislation. Protesters are moving into certain selected forest areas. Already a highly controversial issue . . .

The bed was blissfully comfortable, the warm breeze blew through the open window with more than a hint of the ocean on its breath. The paper dropped from her hands, her eyelids drooped. As she drifted into sleep, her last thought was that she hadn't thought of Arthur Smith once since arriving at Timberlands. Incredible!

It had been a golden day, but the shadows were lengthening. A stronger breeze rattled the slatted blinds of the guest room, but that wasn't what woke Ellie. She'd slept heavily and, at first, she thought the voices were part of a dream. They were familiar, yet unfamiliar — one male and one female, almost outside her window. She struggled to clear her sleep-fogged brain.

The woman's voice was sharp. 'I saw her in the plane. There's somebody else here, isn't there? You know I can't stand that.'

Ellie sat up. There was a faint echo from the morning — the figure from the jetty. 'Rodd,' the voice called out, but there was no sweetness in the voice now. It was bitter, and somehow, off-key — disjointed. 'Why do you have to bring people here? I only want you — '

'Donna!' It was Rodd's voice, but with a quality Ellie hadn't heard before. He was pleading! 'I can't be here all the time. And where've you been all day? I was so pleased when I saw you there to meet me — '

'But you've brought someone with you. That's why I ran away. I wanted to stay out in the woods all night.'

'But would you, Donna? Are you sure you wouldn't have gone to Amanda's? Did you go to Amanda's at all today?'

Ellie froze. It was a private conversation and she shouldn't be listening, but if she got up and shut the window, they'd hear. She tried putting her hands to her ears, but the jagged voice pierced through.

'You won't know, so it doesn't matter what I say . . . '

Ellie pulled a pillow over her head. It was dreadful. The voice was that of a spiteful child's, tormenting the adult.

Was it Rodd's wife? Was she deranged? Pity, regret and sorrow filled Ellie in equal measure. Was this the key to Rodd's brooding anger, his preoccupation? The logging problems at Dalton Island were surely of little significance compared to this.

The voice went on and on, relentlessly accusing Rodd of neglect, indifference, cruelty. His own protest died until he was silent, and Ellie could feel in that silence a despair ill-suited to his powerful character. The voice stopped and Ellie cautiously slid off the bed — if she could get to the shower —

Halfway across the room, she froze, then, in horror, ran into the bathroom, turning both taps at full gush. Even over that sound, the other sound dominated, fainter, but still striking terror to the mind in its utter despair.

It was Donna, now weeping helplessly, long, pitiful sobs, then muffled, and Ellie knew Rodd had put his arms round the hysterical girl and had gathered her into the strong protection of his body.

The bath was practically overflowing as Ellie turned off the taps. She listened, but now there was no sound outside. With a long exhalation of relief, she lay back in the hot tub, but it was some minutes before she stopped shaking. All she could think of, or feel, was a wrenching pity for Rodd Pallister, and his Uncle Ted, who helped to share the burden imposed by Donna Pallister — for Ellie was now convinced that the tormented girl outside on the deck was Rodd's wife.

At first, Ellie thought she'd plead a headache and stay in her room. Knowing she was the cause of Donna's misery made it difficult for her to face supper, but she guessed the girl wouldn't come out anyway, and the golden evening outside beckoned.

As the sun began to set, a soft glow of faint rose suffused the living-room. As Ellie went through, towards the terrace leading to the shore, she paused by the patio doors. On the wall opposite, the sun's rays fingered a picture, lighting up the scene of a North London square, alive with market bustle.

'Why, that's it!' Her surprise spoke out loud. 'It's home. Unbelievable!'

'It's well placed to catch the light, don't you think? Dad loved it. It reminded him of happy times in England. Do you want a drink?' Rodd stood behind her, looking over her shoulder at the canvas. 'We could be there — see, there's a small girl with your colouring and a boy!'

Ellie couldn't turn to face him, he was so close to her, but his voice was, as usual, deep and confident. She moved sideways, turning to look at him. He was smiling, first at her, then at the picture. There was no stress, nor sign of tension, nor the despair she'd heard a short time ago. She began to think that the exchanges she'd heard may have been part of her dreams — but that wasn't possible — the emotion had been too real.

'Isn't it a coincidence — that picture? And both of us here. Did you say 'yes' to a drink?'

'Yes, it is, and no, not now, thanks. I was just going for a walk along the shoreline. I — I slept this afternoon, and I need waking up.'

'I'll come with you. Ted's coping with supper. Anna left the basics, but it'll be later than usual. And I'd like to show you something.'

She followed him across a long sweep of grass towards the shingled tideline. The sun had almost disappeared, but the pink glow still lit up the sea, making black-humped silhouettes of the neighbouring islands.

Rodd put his hand on her arm. 'Over there — look — on the rocks. They come here every evening.'

'What? Those birds? What are they?'

'Bald-headed eagles. We get lots of them along here.'

'But — they're — well, just great brown birds.'

'Look up. Those birds on the rocks,

they're the young. The adults are different. See — they'll swoop down in a moment.'

Then she saw them — white, powerful, heads thrust forward, wing spans wide, fierce autocrats of the skies, sure of their territory.'

'They're magnificent,' she breathed, as the adult birds settled near the young, quite close to where she and Rodd were standing.

'They come down at dusk, and always in the early morning. They're pretty common here, and even more so on Dalton Island. It's ironical, but the baldheaded eagle's very rare in the United States, yet it's their national bird. They'd give a lot to have them in these sort of numbers.'

'Why do they come here?'

Rodd shrugged. 'We've protected them, I suppose. Look, there they go.'

With a great flap of wings, they all soared into the darkening air, hovered a while, then wheeled away towards the forest tops. The sight of the free, wild birds moved Ellie so much she felt a constriction in her throat. Rodd's hand was still on her arm.

'They're free,' she said, 'to come and go as they please — anywhere.' Her voice shook, and Rodd looked at her curiously.

'Ellie, what's the matter? You're not a prisoner.'

'I am.' Quite why she felt so forlorn, she didn't know. It was an alien weakness which she put down to the dramas of the past few days. She felt that if ever there was a caged bird, she was it.

Rodd put his arms around her shoulder. 'Ellie? We have to talk. What Ted said was nonsense. I wouldn't use you to get information on the protesters. Believe me, I had that organised long before you appeared on the scene. Ted's out of touch, and has a vivid imagination. You're going to Dalton Island simply because you'll be safer there. It's remote and quiet, or, at least, it was. It's just unfortunate that it's attracting publicity now, because of the conservationist campaign. But you have to trust me.'

In the almost dark, in the shelter of his arm, Ellie believed him. She remembered his concern and anguish for Donna. Rodd Pallister, tough, masculine, frequently domineering, had another, softer side to his character. She had to believe in his integrity — but she had no right to the comfort of his arms — that was something which belonged to Donna Pallister.

Ellie moved away. She was beginning to trust him, but as for herself . . .

'Rodd,' she said quickly, 'I couldn't help overhearing, this afternoon — you and Donna, outside my room. She sounded so — so — '

'I'm sorry you heard. We were inside her room, but voices carry here.' His voice was as sombre as the blackening night. 'She had a particularly bad day. It's not always like that.'

'Is it because I'm here?'

'Partly. Nothing to do with you

personally. Just — anyone she doesn't know coming to the house. He turned to face the ocean, a tall, black shape against the sky. His stance didn't invite questions. Abruptly, he said, 'Since our parents died, she's been a lot worse.'

Ellie's brain registered his words. 'Donna isn't your wife?'

Rodd turned to stare at her. It was his turn to be astonished. 'My wife! Of course not. Donna's my sister. What gave you that idea?'

'I just assumed it, I suppose.'

'That kind of assumption, Miss Jones, could lead to all sorts of misunderstandings. As it is, I'm still free to do this.' He turned her to him, and kissed her. It was a light, friendly kiss, with the merest hint of something held back, but Ellie couldn't see his expression — it was too dark.

He took her hand, and it was warm and comforting. 'Come on, Ted'll be waiting. Supper should be ready now.'

'But Donna? What's wrong with her?'

His grip tightened. 'Don't worry, you

won't see her this evening. I should think you've had enough of my sister for one day. I'd rather hear about you. You assumed I was married. What about you? I assume you're not, but you must have a — a partner in London?'

Ellie shook her head. 'No. I did have, but he, Ben, that is, decided he didn't want a serious commitment.'

'And you?'

'I thought I did want commitment, but when we split up, it was strange. It didn't hurt much at all. I think we were a habit — a classic case of the boy next door. It seemed that we'd known each other for ever. It was comfortable, like a pair of old socks, I suppose.'

Rodd's burst of laughter startled a pair of night birds which flapped out of the bushes with outraged squawks. 'I love your honesty, and I know the feeling. Old socks can be very comfortable. You don't sound at all bitter about it.'

'I'm not.' Ellie wondered whether she

could ask Rodd a similar question, but he pre-empted her.

'I was engaged to the girl next door, too.' He stopped, and pointed to the right of Timberlands. 'You can't see the house from here, it's well hidden by the trees, but that's where Amanda lived.'

'What happened?'

'We were both young. Eight years ago, and just before the wedding, she went to Europe for a final fling.'

He paused, debating whether to continue. It was all in the past, but the terrible legacy that trip had left was still with him.

'Amanda stayed in Europe, that's all,' he finished flatly.

'But, didn't she ever come back?' Ellie was intrigued.

They reached the house, and could see Ted in the living-room.

Rodd, about to slide back the patio door, looked down at her. 'Oh, yes, Amanda came back — unfortunately.'

6

There was neither sight nor sound of Donna that evening, nor through the night, although Ellie shut her windows and drew her curtains.

Just after dawn, she went down to the shoreline to see if the eagles were there. It was a perfect, spring morning. The water was calm, and the rising sun promised heat later. Several of the young, brownish birds, looking even larger than the adults, were perched on the rocks grooming themselves, but only two mature eagles soared in the sky. Ellie watched them, knowing that she had to photograph them. Rodd had promised there'd be more eagles on Dalton Island which she could use for her feature on the birds in their natural coastal forest habitats.

To Ellie, they symbolised freedom, a freedom she'd always taken for granted before. Now, in spite of what Rodd said, hers had been curtailed, and she wouldn't easily be able to leave Dalton Island. In London, the trial of Arthur Smith would almost certainly put further constraints on her. She tried to put it out of her mind; it was easy out here in the calm tranquillity of the gulf islands. She couldn't wait to start work.

'See you later, eagles,' she called softly to the distant birds, before she went back to the house for breakfast.

Breakfast was liquid only — fruit juice and coffee. Rodd was impatient to be off, and Ellie heard him tell Ted he'd been in to see Donna and that she was still sleeping. 'I'll be back at the week-end,' he added, 'and then we'll have to make a decision. I'll phone, but tell Anna and Buck, only one at a time on the mainland, and for goodness' sake, keep her away from Amanda.' His tone changed. 'Ellie, ready? Glad to see you're travelling light.'

'I don't tend to carry many extras. The photographic gear's heavy enough.'

Ted was reluctant to let Ellie go. 'I've sure enjoyed your visit. I wish it could have been longer. Be certain to come back here.'

'I'd like to,' Ellie said, with mixed feelings.

They took off in Rodd's sea-plane, flying northward over Vancouver Island, and this time, she made no attempt to take pictures. She used her eyes, and filed away the images in her brain. Rodd had promised her he'd fly her over the islands whenever she wanted. There was so much to absorb, so many new scenes and impressions. She put aside personal dilemmas, concentrating on the professional. The aerial view Rodd showed her was the broad context of her work for Conservation Planet. He edged the plane westwards, following the coastline, where settlements were more sparse than on the eastern side.

He raised his voice over the engine noise. 'You can see from here. Large areas have been stripped from the mountains. See, to the east there, that bald looking hill? That's where clear cutting's been allowed, and erosion's followed.'

'It's so ugly.' Ellie saw that the natural, dark-green beauty of the forest had turned black and barren in great swathes. 'No wonder people protest!'

'There are two sides to most arguments, as no doubt you'll find out before long. You heard Bob. He's at one end of the spectrum. Advocates logging the forests — with control. He hates all protesters. Thinks they're all anarchists.'

'And where do you stand?'

'Well, it's difficult. I can see both sides. Down here now, looks terrible from up here, but you get down on the ground, and you'll see new growth. The cut areas will remain virgin, to grow again as forests, and we're learning new techniques all the time. There are all sorts of compromises to consider.'

He gave Ellie a rueful grin. 'Trouble is, trees and wildlife can be a mite wayward, and won't always fit in with man's plans. Eagles use a series of three nests, so now, instead of leaving one tree for them, we leave four hundred metres of uncut forest. Giant cedar-woods need one hundred and twenty years to grow — too slow for my Japanese buyers!'

He pulled the plane away from Vancouver Island, swinging further west.

'Don't look so serious, Ellie. You aren't going to solve this one in the time you're here. Look and learn. You'll find a viewpoint, and it'll resolve itself somehow. In the future it has to.'

Ellie was amazed how laid-back Rodd appeared on the issue. Surely it was terribly important to him. Timber was his livelihood.

'There's Dalton Island. And there's my ancient forest — on the north side. I'll show it to you while you're here. It's exactly as it was eight hundred years ago. It'd make good material for an article for Conservation Planet. Hold on. I might just hit some loose timber in the water. It can be a tricky landing.'

He didn't. The little plane bounced gently to a small jetty, made from a few raw logs, lashed together. Rodd switched off the engine and swung himself out. Balancing precariously on the floats, he ducked around the front of the plane to the passenger side and opened her door.

'But — I thought we were going to the town. There's nothing here at all.'

'Salt Creek's hardly a town. You'll see later. Look around — and don't dare call this nothing!' He held out his arms to help her down, and for an instant Ellie was held against his strong body. Then she stepped on to the logs which wobbled so much she was thrust back into his arms.

'Careful, or you'll be in the water. Better still — ' He picked her up and, with a sure-footed athletic stride, carried her across the landing stage, over the rocks, and on to a sandy beach. He held on to her, looking deeply into her eyes.

Ellie held her breath, trying to fathom his intent. He swung her round slowly, in a full circle, holding her out as though she were a ballerina. She felt featherlight in his arms, and saw what he wanted her to see.

The sea-plane had docked in a perfect cove, a tiny inlet of sand and rock hollowed out of the base of a steep, forest-clad cliff. The water was clear and deep, reflecting the dense vegetation surrounding it. The beach faced south, trapping the sun's warmth.

'You call this nothing?' Rodd smiled as he put her down on the warm sand. 'It's my private, and very personal, picnic spot. I've an hour or so before I have to fly back to Vancouver. We can swim before lunch.'

'Lunch!'

'A picnic. I brought food in the plane.'

Ellie drew a breath. Rodd Pallister was full of surprises. When she first met him the surprises had all been bad, but now, well, things were beginning to look up — she could have fallen into worse hands! A feeling of delight threatened to shorten her breath even more. She temporised. 'I don't have a swim-suit, and, won't the water be cold at this time of the year?'

'Freezing. But it'll be worth it. If you're modest, there's a bikini in the plane.'

'You've thought of everything.' Ellie wondered whom the bikini belonged to. Donna? Even Amanda? Did he still see her? Someone as attractive as Rodd must have a string of girl friends. She remembered the girl in the restaurant in Vancouver.

His grey eyes held hers. 'You can swim naturally of course. No-one can visit this beach, except by boat or plane. It's a rugged hike from inland.' His glance burned through her.

'I'd prefer the bikini, if you don't mind.'

The white bikini fitted her perfectly. The sea was icy cold, but pure and invigorating. Ellie was a strong swimmer and matched Rodd stroke for stroke as they swam together out of the cove and round the base of the high cliffs. It was too cold to stay long, and Ellie ran up the beach gasping for breath. Rodd threw her a towel, but the sun was high in the sky, strong and warming.

'That was wonderful.' She shook her wet hair like a dog. 'First swim of the year.'

'Do you swim in England?'

'Yes, but indoors mainly. Thanks for bringing me here. It's beautiful.'

'It's the best introduction to Dalton Island I could think of. Not too much like prison!'

Did he have to remind her? For a few moments she'd felt as though she was on a magic holiday — with an ideal companion.

'You've got to remember, Ellie, although you're not a prisoner, you are in hiding. I told you, Dalton's safer than anywhere, but if the logging protest does focus here, then there will be a lot of publicity. If that happens we'll think again, and maybe move on to the next island, Corag. The problem is, there's hardly anything there but wildlife.'

'Sounds ideal.' Ellie bit her lip, and shivered.

Rodd squatted on the sand beside her and put his arm around her shoulders.

'Don't worry, you'll be safe here. It was too risky in Vancouver — the drug gangs are well established there, but although the problem's spread to some of the islands, it's not hit Dalton yet — as far as we know.' His face was grim, and Ellie felt as though the sun had gone in. 'Just keep a low profile. Pete Winthrop, manager of the saw-mill, will keep an eye on you. His wife runs a small bed and breakfast place. She'll take care of you. You'll like Sally.'

He got up. 'Let's eat — and — um — maybe you should take off that wet swimsuit.' He spoke casually, but his eyes were soft as he looked at her attractive body in the brief bikini.

The holiday mood returned during the picnic. Rodd had brought cold chicken, salad and a vacuum flask of the Pallister speciality, fish chowder. The air and the swim had made Ellie hungry.

'There's wine if you want it. I'll stick to fruit juice. I'll be flying back to Vancouver soon.'

Ellie's stomach did a downward flip. She'd grown used to Rodd's strong presence, in spite of her early resentment. She felt safe when he was with her.

'No wine, thanks. This is perfect.' She leaned back against a sun-warmed rock and closed her eyes, savouring the moment, before she asked, 'Isn't your business on Dalton Island? The sawmill?'

'It's one of them.' Rodd's voice was lazy, languorous. Ellie was aware of his muscled brown shoulders, so very close to hers. 'But I operate from Vancouver City mostly. I'm away a lot.'

'What else do you do?'

'Is this the investigative journalist speaking? It's business, Ellie. Mostly quite mundane stuff. Selling my timber, making deals — '

'You enjoy it?'

He turned his head to look at her, and through closed eyes, she felt his scrutiny. 'Not always — but one day I aim to build a house here, on Dalton Island, quit travelling, stay home, fish and sail, just like Uncle Ted.'

'A family home? For Uncle Ted — and Donna?' The air was still, and as soon as she'd said it, Ellie wished she hadn't.

'Maybe.' But his voice was flat. The spell was broken. 'I'll take the things back to the plane. We must get moving.'

'Can I help?'

'No. Stay there. Enjoy the sun — while it lasts.'

He was curt, abrupt, and Ellie wished she could recall her inconsequential remark about Donna. She sighed, and sank farther down on to the sand, soaking up the sun. It would be easy to fall asleep . . .

A shadow came between Ellie and the sun. Sleepily, she smiled. It must be Rodd. Time to go. She opened her eyes — and screamed. It wasn't Rodd. A tall figure in black jeans and T-shirt stood over her. He wore a red headband, with dark hair tied back in a pony-tail. He carried a rifle, and his smile was not pleasant. Ellie struggled to her feet.

'No, don't get up. You make a very pretty picture down there. Beauty on the beach!'

'Who . . . ?'

Ellie's nervous question was drowned by Rodd's powerful roar, as he ran down the beach. 'Who are you? How did you get here?' Rodd shouted.

The man was not in the least perturbed. His grin was impudent, his voice confident. 'Easy. I saw the sea-plane. I watched it dip down, then I simply followed my nose. You must be Rodd Pallister.'

'How — ' Rodd growled, but the man interrupted.

'I saw your logo! It's not very difficult

to spot it on your plane.'

Rodd took a step towards the intruder. Ellie stood up in alarm. Rodd's fists were clenched. His voice was deadly. 'You are on private property. Get off, before I throw you off.'

The man raised his eyebrows. 'Difficult,' he murmured. 'Besides, I do have a right to be here. I'm working — '

'With a gun!' Rodd snapped. 'You go back the way you came — or — '

'Or what, Mr Pallister? You'd look pretty foolish throwing one of your own employees off the island.'

Rodd's eyes narrowed. 'My employee?'

'Yup. Pete Winthrop, your manager, hired me last week. Sent me out today up the hillside to check out the road erosion. That's when I saw your plane.' He glanced at Ellie and, with a barely-concealed leer, added, 'A very private place to bring a girl. Pity I stumbled on it, by accident, of course!'

Ellie looked nervously at the two men. The tension was explosive. Rodd looked ready to grind the fellow into the rock — but the man had a gun.

He saw Ellie's eyes on it, and touched it casually. 'Don't worry, miss. A hunting rifle. Never know what you'll meet in the woods. Bears — '

'You need my permission to carry that.' Rodd was visibly trying to control himself.

'I have my own licence, but Pete OK'd it, too. My name's Rufus Stone. Pleased to met you, Mr Pallister. I assume you are Mr Pallister?'

Rodd nodded curtly, but his face was grim. 'You say Pete hired you last week? To do what? Are you a logger? And where are you from? I've never seen you around here before. We employ only local labour.'

'I've worked in timber before, in Oregon, in the States. And Pete seemed to be short of an odd-job man, so he took me on.'

Rufus Stone's reply was smooth, too smooth, Rodd thought, but if his manager had hired him, there must be a good reason, and he was beginning to have a shrewd suspicion he might know why. He allowed his anger to evaporate, but not his suspicions. 'I suppose you have identity card with you?'

'Sure do.' Rufus dug into the pocket of his jeans, and showed his plastic covered picture and details.

Rodd scanned it briefly before handing it back. 'OK. You should wear it. There are a lot of strangers on the island.'

'So I've noticed.' The reply was casual.

'I'll check with Pete when I get back. But you've still no business down here, employee or not. If you're checking the roads, that's what you should be doing. This beach is a long way from the road.'

'Sorry, boss.' From his expression, Rufus Stone was anything but sorry, and Ellie felt Rodd's impatient anger begin to simmer. 'I found a cut-through when I was checking out some fallen timber,' he offered.

'I suggest you find your way back to the road then — and remember, this is a private beach. There's nothing here connected with your job. Come on, Ellie. I don't have much time.'

'Is the young lady a Pallister employee, too?' Rufus asked.

Before Rodd's anger could explode, Ellie intercepted, 'I can answer for myself, Mr Stone. I'm not employed by Pallister's. I'm on Dalton Island for Conservation Planet, if you must know.'

Rufus Stone's eyes narrowed. 'What are you doing here for them?'

Rodd's anger exploded. 'It's got absolutely nothing to do with you. Now, get off this beach and get back to work, or your employment with Pallister's will be very short lived.'

Rufus Stone threw a baleful glance at Rodd, and his grip on his rifle tightened. The antagonism between them was electric.

Rufus was the first to back off. 'Sorry again,' he muttered. 'I'm going. Can I give you a lift?' he said to Ellie. 'The Jeep's not far away.' He knew he was pushing his luck, but if the girl was working for Conservation Planet, he had to know what she was going to do. He saw Rodd's expression and decided that discretion, on this occasion, was the right course.

'All right, I'm going. Nice to meet you, Mr Pallister. You, too, miss. I hope to see you in Salt Creek.' He lifted his hand in an ironic wave and ran lightly back into the dense undergrowth.

'I might have liked a ride back to Salt Creek,' Ellie said, resentful that Rodd hadn't even consulted her.

'No, you wouldn't. Not with him. I don't trust him, and besides, I told you — a low profile — and that doesn't include picking up with strangers and riding off into the wilderness with them. For Pete's sake, learn some commonsense.'

He bent to pick up the towels. 'Come on, I've got to get to Vancouver.'

'Just a minute.' Ellie's resentment began to boil. 'You seem to think I can't take a step without your permission — but you just remember, this is voluntary, and I can leave here at any time I want to, and go back to London. I don't have to take orders from you, or anyone else. I daresay Conservation Planet could find me another part of the world to hide in.' She glared defiantly at Rodd who stood, beach towels dangling from his hand, looking down at her.

His jaw tightened, and his eyes hardened. Dropping the towels, he took a step towards her. Ellie stood her ground. Then, in one swift movement, he swept her into his arms and brought his mouth hard down on hers.

With a gasp of shock, Ellie resisted briefly, but Rodd's strength was formidable — and she was aware of an answering need in her own body. Weakly, she clung to him, as he kissed her with a sweet passion which also had more than a touch of impatient anger.

Rufus Stone, in his ascent back to where he'd left his Jeep, saw the two figures moulded together, and nodded his head in satisfaction. This was going to be an interesting assignment.

7

It was only a short flight over the island to Salt Creek, the main settlement. It's small harbour had several docking stages, two already occupied by sea-planes.

'We use them like buses,' Rodd said laconically as he helped Ellie out. 'You must learn to fly while you're here.'

Oh, sure, she thought — anything else? Still shaken by the impact of Rodd's kiss, she was having a hard task trying to maintain an ice-cool, aloof persona. Neither of them had said a word on the short flight. On the beach, Rodd had released her, stared at her darkly for a moment, then boarded the plane. Ellie was left to gather up the towels and follow.

He transferred her luggage to a Jeep, parked by the stage, and drove away from the harbourside, across a broad expanse of Tarmac, into a yard stacked high with timber.

'This is the business part of Salt Creek — saw and pulp mill, and port. Farther up the road it's a lot prettier, and there's a small marina. There are company sail boats you can borrow if you want to explore the coastline. You can use this Jeep, and Pete will show you around.' He stopped in front of a large, wooden office building.

'Won't you be back at all?' Ellie tried to keep her voice neutral.

He handed her the keys to the Jeep. 'You can hang on to my keys. I shan't need them for a day or two. I'll be back, but I'm not sure when. Pete will keep you in touch. Here he is. Hi!'

A craggy giant of a man, with a thick shock of blond hair, ran down the steps of the building. With both hands outstretched, his greeting couldn't have been warmer.

'Rodd! Good to see you. I saw the plane come in.' He turned curious eyes on Ellie. 'This must be Ellie. Hi, there.

Great to have you on Dalton. Sally's coming along to pick you up.'

His grip was warm and friendly, and Ellie took an instant liking to him. 'Oh, dear, won't that be a bother? Rodd says I can use the Jeep.'

'Won't hear of it. That's no way to treat a guest, especially a friend of Rodd's. Sally's dying to meet you. Course, she's really coming to see Rodd.' His voice was teasing. 'She's disappointed he's not staying for supper at least.'

'I'm sorry, too, but I'm meeting the Tokyo crowd this afternoon. Can't be late for them.'

Brakes screeched and a battered, old pick-up came to a halt inches from their feet.

'That sounds like Sally, now. She never can do things quietly.'

A plump, pretty red-head swirled out of the vehicle, flung her arms round Rodd, kissed her husband, and took Ellie's hands — all in one rapid movement.

'You're a skunk, Rodd Pallister, not stopping a while. Never mind — all the better for us to get to know Ellie on her own. Jump in. I've left some pies in the oven. See you at suppertime, Pete. Don't be late, and oh, there's a whole load of new folk arrived on the ferry, and they're not tourists. Looks like trouble to me. They've even got their placards ready. The 'Save Our Trees' brigade,' she explained to Ellie. 'They've been trickling in lately, and the natives don't like it. How about your luggage?'

'In the Jeep,' Ellie said, knowing that she was going to like Sally. She turned to Rodd. 'Thanks for bringing me here, and for your help with everything.'

He shrugged. 'That's OK. It's in my interests, too, that you turn in good copy for Conservation Planet. I was officially briefed to help you, don't forget. I just didn't reckon on such — er — close involvement.' He took her hand in a formal handshake. 'Enjoy the island. Good luck, and remember — a low profile.'

He and Pete went into the office, Sally impatiently gunning the engine, but not before Ellie overheard Rodd say, 'What's this about you taking on a new man — Rufus Stone? He looks like he could be trouble . . . '

A sense of desolation squeezed Ellie's heart. He was right — there was no need for close involvement. That would never lead anywhere. She'd come to British Columbia to work and that's exactly what she'd do.

★   ★   ★

Sally and Pete laid on a welcome-to-Dalton supper for her, inviting a few of their friends from the town to join them. The one obstacle which might have created tension was cleared immediately by Sally's forthright announcement at supper, when she introduced Ellie to the rest of the guests.

'Ellie's from Conservation Planet so, I'm afraid, maybe that puts us on the opposite side of the fence, apart from Dorrie here, who's my best friend in town, in spite of her kookie ideas about saving owls and eagles.'

Dorrie, a slight, dark girl who looked barely out of her teens, giggled. 'They are not kookie ideas. I just believe you should think a bit harder about ruining the environment. Once you've sold your forests, spoiled the salmon streams and made the birds extinct, what've you got left here?'

'Dorrie owns a gallery and gift shop on the marina. She actually wants to attract tourists to Dalton Island!'

Tourists! Ellie looked alarmed. That meant the outside world. She was meant to be in hiding.

'Don't listen to Sally. If we do have a tourist season here, it's pretty short lived, I can tell you. A few weeks at most. But the islands are attracting more and more artists, and people from the mainland who want to retire here, or simply escape the rat race.' Dorrie smiled across at Ellie. 'Conservation

Planet's a great organisation. I'd be proud to work for it.'

'I am, but I don't have to follow their philosophies slavishly. Of course, I agree with conserving and preserving the environment, but as to the logging issue here, I don't know enough about it yet to have an objective view point.'

'Well.' Pete looked round the supper table. 'You'll find that most people here, apart from Dorrie, are all for sensible and controlled harvesting of the forests. We can't just stop, to save spotted owls and eagles. Times are bad enough as it is. The timber industry's laying off men all the time.'

'We should expand tourism and fishing. Diversify — that's progress.'

Ellie could see that Dorrie was getting heated, and an older guest was obviously steaming for a fight.

He pointed his fork at Dorrie. 'I'm a darn sight older than you, and I know what unemployment does to a small community like ours. Rodd Pallister and his dad have always looked after us, giving us good jobs — a good living. If these weirdos who are coming into Dalton try anything, or, if they want confrontation, you can put me down as a volunteer for COPITT.'

'COPITT?' Ellie asked. 'Whatever does that stand for?'

He was pleased to give her an answer. Stabbing his fork in the air to emphasise every word, he said slowly, 'Citizens On Patrol In The Trees. And I've got my own gun licence, too, like most folk around here.'

'Now, Jim, you'll be frightening Ellie back to England with that kind of talk. How about telling her about the Logging Festival next week. That's usually a good time. A real friendly affair. Don't want to spoil that, now, do we?'

Jim looked as though he would like to do just that, but aware he was an invited guest, subsided into his supper.

★   ★   ★

Ellie remembered that discussion a week later, when she was sorting out all the material she'd gathered since arriving on Dalton Island. She'd thoroughly enjoyed the week. Arthur Smith, drugs, gangs, all had stayed well in the back of her mind. Instead, Dalton Island, with its tranquil waters, dense vegetation and sparkling streams, had completely captivated her.

Up at dawn every day, she was out recording and noting. Pete acted as her guide on occasion, or some of the more experienced loggers, but often she went on her own. She loved the quiet dignity of the soaring forests, hated to see the cleared, barren stretches, with broken stumps of what had once been magnificent cedars.

Pete had told her that Rodd's management strategy was to plant four trees for every one cut down. Mistakes had been made in the past, but Rodd was trying to put them right. But the world was hungry for timber. If they didn't supply it, some other country would.

After a day or so, Ellie sorted out the loggers and the timber men from the conservationists and protesters. By day the small town was quiet. The loggers worked, the conservationists hiked the nature trails or stayed at home in their camp sites. At first, they were just a few; a couple of camper vans, and half a dozen tents. Gradually, the numbers more than quadrupled, the tents multiplied, and the number of vans increased.

In the town, there were some suspicious murmurings.

'They should be moved on.'

'What are they up to?'

Inevitably, they were blamed for everything that went wrong. Even an unseasonable and violent night thunderstorm was said to be the work of a tree witch who wandered the forests, marking tree trunks with phosphorous paint.

Ellie watched the growing tension uneasily, aware how quickly small town gossip and prejudice could turn to bigotry and persecution. Photo journalist as she was, she didn't relish witnessing a potential disaster when people could be hurt. The tree and eagle people, as they were dubbed, because of their fondness for quoting statistics about the relationship of trees to eagles, seemed harmless and friendly, showing no sign of violence or vandalism. Town and conservationists co-existed harmoniously. Until the day of the forest fire . . .

Late one afternoon, ten days after Ellie's arrival, a patch of forest caught fire. It was quickly dealt with. Forest fires were dreaded by timbermen, but the company fire service was one hundred per cent efficient, and little damage was caused. The fire itself would normally have rated minimum comment, but a rumour spread, much faster than the fire, that it had been deliberately started by the tree and eagle people. Why the tree people, dedicated to saving trees, should deliberately burn them down, wasn't discussed. The fire provided a handy focus for those people who wanted the hippies off the island.

And there was another element now amongst the peaceable conservationists. Daily, the ferry brought more anti-loggers on to the island. They didn't come in camper vans or with large, family tents. The newcomers had minimum back-packs, slept rough in the woods, and looked tough.

On the evening of the fire, Rufus Stone telephoned Ellie. She'd seen him around the town, and he'd nodded, but made no attempt to speak. She was surprised, when she answered the phone, to find him on the line.

'Hi there. Rufus Stone. I thought it was time to renew our acquaintance, now you're settled in. How about a drink tonight?'

'I don't think — '

'Don't refuse, Ellie. There are some things on the island I'd like to show you which could be useful in your work for Conservation Planet. I've noticed you around with your camera.'

'I'm afraid I've got a lot of work to do tonight.'

'It'll keep until tomorrow. All work and no play . . . '

Ellie hesitated. There was something about Rufus Stone she didn't like. His face had remained in her memory as a face worth photographing — piratical — fanatical — demon-driven! She was intrigued, too, by the way he had stood up to Rodd, on the beach. He was no ordinary, odd-job timberman. His voice was persuasive, soft and dark, and she hadn't heard from Rodd at all. Just a word via Pete that Rodd hoped everything was going well, and that he was tied up with family business right now.

'OK, just for an hour. Where shall I meet you?'

'I'll pick you up. Fifteen minutes.'

It was thus that Ellie was a first-hand witness to the violence that almost engulfed Salt Creek in a riot of unmanageable proportions for its two police officers. As it was, the only cell in the somewhat grandly-named town jail was insufficient to cope with those arrested, and a local hall was commandeered to take the overflow.

Pete didn't like the idea of Ellie going out with Rufus Stone, and made no bones about saying so, but when he said, 'What'll Rodd say?' it made Ellie all the more determined to go.

'It's none of his business, and he isn't showing much interest in my movements at present,' she said briskly, then relented when she saw Pete's worried expression. 'I'll be back within the hour. You mustn't worry.'

Sally was on Ellie's side. 'Don't be such an old prune, Pete. We're not Ellie's jailers.'

Rufus called for her in a very old, very comfortable Cadillac.

'Some car,' she said, eyeing the maroon monster.

'Can't afford to go far in it. Costs about a dollar a yard to run!'

'Should we walk then?'

'A lady like you — on the streets of Salt Creek? Wouldn't hear of it. I only bought this today, just with you in mind.'

Ellie looked at him sceptically. He was flirting with her! She wasn't sure whether she liked it or not, but it made a change from staying in and working.

'Where are we going?'

'Depends whether you want local colour, or the smart, new restaurant by the ferry landing.'

'Local colour, please.'

Afterwards, Ellie was always to wonder what would have happened had she chosen the smart restaurant option, but Rufus Stone was shrewd. Even on the fleeting acquaintance of the beach encounter, he was almost certain she'd opt for local colour. And he very much wanted her to witness what was bound to happen. And she would, as long as Judd and his friends did their stuff — and they'd never failed him before.

He parked the Cadillac on the waterfront, where there were two bars, and ushered Ellie into the larger of the two. She'd actually been in once before with Sally for a lunchtime drink. Then it had been quiet, empty, and very pleasant. Now, it was smoke filled — smoke with an unmistakable tang — ear-shatteringly noisy, and very full.

'Local colour,' Rufus said firmly, elbowing his way to a couple of stools. He seemed to know lots of people, two of whom obligingly slid off the stools when he and Ellie approached. 'Drink?'

'White wine, please. Dry.'

He nodded, as though that was what he'd expected, and she wished she'd asked for something less obviously feminine. He ordered a soft drink for himself.

'Cheers.' He raised his glass to her. 'How's the work coming?'

Ellie tried to answer, but the noise level was rising. It was impossible to talk. She shouted, 'Very well,' turned to look around the bar, and instinctively ducked as a bottle was hurled across the room.

At the same time, Rufus grabbed her arm, pulled her off her stool, and jostled her through a door by the end of the bar.

'Looks like trouble. I wouldn't want you hurt. Quick, follow me up the stairs.'

Up the stairs, across the landing, and they were in what must have been a sail loft in the old days. It had a window at one end which looked directly down on to the bar.

'Good grief, what's going on?' Ellie wished she had her camera with her, then was ashamed of herself. It really looked very nasty down there. Bottles, glasses and fists flew in all directions. It was like a scene from every Western movie she'd ever seen.

'Seems the good townsfolk of Dalton Island have turned on the protesters.'

'How do you know that?' Ellie said defensively.

'Look for yourself. Who's attacking who? Ouch! See that girl the old guy's knocked over? She's a tree-and-eagle lady. Bad feeling from the fire maybe.'

'Someone should call the police.' Even as she spoke, sirens wailed outside.

'There's only one police car on the island, so it looks as though they've called the fire service out, too. They won't be too pleased, especially after having to deal with the forest fire.'

'We can't just stay here and watch.'

'No option — unless you want to get involved.'

'But why are they doing this?'

'It was an inevitable confrontation, I'm afraid. The loggers want to keep their jobs, rather than keep the forests. The protesters want to keep the forests. There's no compromise. One side has to win. Bound to be some damage.'

The firemen used water hoses to keep the fighting under control in the bar, but scuffles continued along the wharf and in the timber yard. Piles of stacked timber were strewn around, and two log trucks were overturned. Ellie and Rufus went downstairs eventually, to see a disgruntled, sodden proprietor cursing 'those tree thugs,' and threatening to get them chased off the island.

'But, how did it start?' she asked.

'Dunno. One minute the loggers were enjoying a hard-earned drink — those damned tree idlers have been here all night — then suddenly, a load more of them come in and set about the loggers. I tell you, I'm just about sick of them.'

Several people had been arrested, and the police officer was still taking statements. A local, freelance reporter, was getting his story together. Ellie and Rufus, dry and uninjured, attracted his attention.

'You two just come in?' he asked. 'You missed a good old scene.'

'No, we saw it all, from up there,' Ellie answered innocently.

'Time we went,' Rufus said quickly, taking her arm.

Ellie, just too late, put her hand up against the photographer's flash.

'Damn,' Rufus cursed.

'Oh, no!' Ellie groaned.

They spoke simultaneously, but for very different reasons.

★ ★ ★

Next morning, the town was divided. Many people were ashamed of the violence, and felt things had gone too far. After all, the conservationists hadn't actually done anything until last night. For some though, resentments burned and scapegoats were looked for.

'Shouldn't Rodd know?' Ellie asked Pete at breakfast.

'He does. I talked to him last night.'

'And?'

'Still tied up,' Pete mumbled through a mouthful of hashbrowns and bacon, 'and there's nothing he can do now. Anyway it's the Logging Festival on Saturday. He's bound to come for that. It'll all have blown over by then, you'll see.'

Ellie sincerely hoped so, but thought Pete was probably over optimistic.

On the Saturday she had to concede

that he'd been right. The Logging Festival, an excuse for a day-long carnival and party, also showed off traditional logging skills. It was held in a large clearing out of town, on the edge of the forest. The stalls, crafts and barbecues attracted everybody in an apparently harmonious mix. It was a friendly, family-outing day. Tree people mixed with townsfolk — after the fight, the rougher element, released from custody, seemed to have left, and the loggers were fully occupied in the competitions for fastest tree felling, fastest tree slicing and fastest tree climbing.

The last one was the most popular. The loggers wore huge, spiked grappling irons on their boots, and shinned up giant cedars at the speed of light. Ellie was also intrigued at the timbermen's own form of darts — where loggers would throw enormous axes — almost too heavy for Ellie even to pick up — at huge targets.

'Just like the old days,' Pete said

happily. 'I told you, Ellie. The other night was just a storm in a teacup, blown out of all proportion.'

Yet Ellie was uneasy. It seemed too good to be true. After the pub brawl, Salt Creek had attracted a few television reporters and newsmen looking for a story. The picture of Ellie and Rufus had appeared in the local paper and to her dismay, its headline ran, **Conservation Planet Girl Looks on as Factions Clash.** It was a blurry picture, and not much like her. She just hoped it wouldn't be featured in the Vancouver Island papers — and that Rodd wouldn't see it. So much for low profile!

The reporters had packed up as the arrested people were released on bail. There was no aftermath. The story was dead, so they all went back to the mainland, grumbling about 'Hicksville.'

Ellie's pleasure at the festival day was marred only by Rodd's continued absence. Sally, too, complained furiously to her husband.

' 'Course he should be here. It's his logging town. He's never missed one before. His father always brought the whole family. Even if they were abroad, they'd all come back for the Logging Festival.'

His family? Ellie's ears pricked up. 'Donna?'

'All of them. Parents, John and Harriet, Cathy, Donna and Rodd, of course.'

'Cathy?'

Sally looked curiously at Ellie. 'Don't you know about his family?'

'No — only Donna. She's sick, isn't she?'

'Yes, but — '

'Honey, I don't think you should talk about Rodd's family,' Pete interrupted. 'He wouldn't like it. You know how sensitive he is.'

'But Ellie's — ' Sally protested.

'No!'

This time it was a command, and Sally shut up.

'He's bound to be here in a day or

so.' Pete tried to make amends.

'How can you be so sure?' It was impossible for Sally to remain squashed for long.

'Don't ask. Confidential. Company business, but I promise, he'll be here.'

'Oh, blast the company. Come on, Ellie, let's get a glass of wine. The bar tent's over there, and we'll get some barbecued chicken. First, the Ladies' tent, before I fill up on wine.'

'It's in the corner, by the trees. I'll come, too.'

On the way to the Ladies' tent, discreetly, but inconveniently sited well away from the main stalls, Ellie glanced towards the forest. The sun was setting and twilight was near. Dark, inky-green trees were like cut-outs against the gold sky. A flash of metal caught her attention, then another.

She moved closer. Sally had gone on ahead. On the dirt road through the forest, Rufus Stone's Cadillac was well camouflaged, but the chrome bumper had reflected the low, evening sun.

Treading quietly, Ellie moved nearer. Rufus was talking to two men in dark suits — certainly not the casual clothes of Salt Creek folk — and he held a mobile phone in his hand. A twig snapping underfoot set a startled bird flapping skywards. The three men looked up, Ellie eased back, and after a few minutes the Cadillac moved off. She didn't think they'd seen her.

*　*　*

After the Logging Festival, the island appeared to settle back into its customary routine, yet Ellie, while continuing to record and photograph, began to sense a subtle change in the timber men. They'd always been unfailingly polite and helpful, and she'd tried not to get in their way too much. They hadn't been very busy — very little actual tree felling had taken place, and there had been talk that Rodd Pallister was losing interest in his logging operation. It was rumoured he'd been to New York, and was in Tokyo now. Some even muttered that the conservationists had scared him off, and that he was planning to sell Dalton Island altogether.

Pete refused to comment, but he, too, had the air of a man who had a secret.

Ellie found it hard to pinpoint the change, but the anti-protester mutterings suddenly ceased. There was an air of expectancy, excitement almost, in the timber yard, and in the forest. The loggers even went out of their way to be friendly with the tree people. It was as though they were waiting for something to happen.

Rufus Stone felt it, too, and it disturbed him. Usually he was two steps ahead of his quarry. He called the shots, and always knew what was going on. He decided it was time for action. He cultivated Ellie, reporting rare bird sightings to her, and offered to take her to photograph a pair of great-horned owls he'd discovered in the forest. She was tempted, but refused. She didn't trust him.

Pete reinforced her suspicions. 'Don't get involved with him in any way. He's a slippery customer.'

'Why don't you get rid of him? I can't see that he does very much work.'

'There are reasons,' was all Pete would say.

Ellie had given up asking about Rodd. It seemed he'd lost interest in her welfare, too. The future was too uncertain to contemplate, so she enjoyed the present, and the island.

A few days after the Logging Festival, the tough young men began to come back to the island, and, while Ellie was out looking for nesting eagles deep in the forest, she encountered Rufus Stone, supposedly checking the salmon streams for silt.

8

Ellie was reloading her camera when she saw the two figures in the distance. She assumed they were loggers, who would be used to her, so she took no notice. It was only when one of the men came nearer that she recognised Rufus.

'Ellie Jones!' He had his rifle, and a bottle of water. He sat down on a mossy rock to take a drink. He held the flask out to her.

'No thanks. What about the other man?'

'What other man? Nobody around but me — and you,' he added pointedly.

'But I saw someone.'

'Imagination. Deer, or elk maybe. There are a few around. I thought you must be taking pictures of them.'

'No. I'm doing the vegetation — the undergrowth. New plants from the dying ones.' She wished he'd go away, but he settled himself more comfortably on the stone and laid his rifle on the ground. His dark eyes were wide, and had a frenetic glint, which made Ellie uneasy. There was an odd quality about him, like a spring, coiled for action. She put her camera in her back pack. 'Must be getting on,' she said as casually as she could.

'No. Stay. I want to talk to you, now I've got you here on your own. Why do you avoid me in Salt Creek?'

'I don't. I'm busy right now. Another time — '

'Now.' He stood up, not exactly barring her way, but making sure she'd have to push past him to stay on the track. 'It won't take long.' He'd come to a decision about Ellie. He needed some publicity, and not just the local rag for this one. First he had to find something out. He sat down again on the rock, indicating that Ellie should join him.

Short of running ignominiously away, she didn't have much option. She wasn't afraid of him — just wary, and a bit puzzled.

Abruptly, he said, 'Rodd Pallister? Is he anything to you?'

'Of course not. Though what it's got to do with you — '

'Good.' He ignored her protest. 'You know he's in Japan?'

'I didn't know, but why should I? I'm here to do a job, that's all.'

'Good,' he repeated, 'and I can help you.'

'How?'

'Listen. I'm going to trust you. We're on the same side. Conservation Planet is for preserving the environment, not gutting it like the Pallisters and their ilk.'

'But I don't — '

'You've seen what's happened here already. Hectares of forest, gone for ever. Precious resources — sold for profit.'

'I haven't seen much actual tree felling. More planting — '

'It's too late for that,' he interrupted.

'And I know they're going to cut down a huge section of timber north of the island. Any day now. Pete Winthrop and his loggers think they're keeping it a secret, but he's made a mistake.'

Ellie remembered Pete's air of excited anticipation. 'How do you know?'

'Never mind. That's not important. You don't think all these conservationists have come to Dalton Island just for a holiday? They want action. They're a protest movement. We want to show we mean business, and we need government legislation to stop the rape of the forests. The government won't do a thing unless we show our intent.'

'What are you going to do?'

'Can I trust you?'

'I — don't know. I've got a duty to the Canadian Government — to the Forestry Commission.'

'You've a duty to your own environment, too, and to Conservation Planet. They're paying you to — '

'To be objective!' Ellie leaped up.

'You'd better not tell me any more, I don't want to hear it.'

Rufus grabbed her arm and pulled her back. 'Sit down! I could make things difficult for you.'

'How?'

'A few phone calls. To Conservation Planet. To the Forestry Commission.'

'Saying what?'

Rufus grinned wolfishly. 'Oh, I'd think of something. I'm very good at sowing seeds — of doubt. I could get you called back to London, and I don't think you'd like that.'

'What do you mean?' Ellie felt a lead lump in her stomach. What did he know? Could he possibly be somehow connected with Arthur Smith? It was a preposterous thought, but the worry niggled. She had no doubt that he could cause trouble.

The grin became an appeased smile. 'But I'd hate to do that, Ellie, because I need your help. I'd much rather we worked as allies — not enemies.'

It was a hot day, but Ellie shivered.

'There's no need to be alarmed. I'll simply tell you what we're going to do, then you can be there to photograph it as it happens — giving maximum publicity. Conservation Planet's own photographer — on the spot!'

'I can't do that,' she protested.

'I think you'll find you can. This is what we're going to do . . . '

Ellie listened in horror, as Rufus calmly told her how he had orchestrated the conservationists in a massive campaign of disruption on the island — starting that very night.

'You've heard of tree spiking? The early evening ferry is bringing more protesters, and they'll be carrying five thousand, ten-centimetre steel nails, which will be driven into the trees designated for cutting. Most of the group are already camped up north. You might have noticed a gradual dwindling of protesters from around Salt Creek. The truce at the logging festival was all meant to lull everyone into a false sense of security. Our supporters left in Salt Creek will take over the mill and yard, and keep out Pallister employees.'

'But that's ridiculous. You'll force a confrontation. The loggers won't let you get away with that.'

'We won't fire the first shots. We never do. It'll be self defence.'

Ellie remembered Jim, on her first night at Sally's. He'd be a very eager vigilante, and probably wouldn't hesitate to fire the first shot.

'Once the trees are spiked, they can't safely go through the saw-mills. The blade hits the steel — and bingo — lots of damage!'

'It's dangerous. Men in the saw-mill could be killed.'

'Of course it's dangerous. That's why we tell the bosses which trees are spiked, so they're no use for felling.'

'You know that the whole community will be put out of work if you do this? And tree spiking's illegal.'

'They'll be out of work soon anyway. As to the spiking — you have to be caught with the hammer in your hand to prove it. When we take over the yard at the end of today's shift, there'll be so much commotion, no-one will be within miles of the tree spikers up north — and they'll be back well before morning. Which reminds me, I must go. Don't forget your camera, Ellie. There should be fun at the yard.'

'What's to stop me going to the police, or Pete Winthrop, now?'

'I'm pretty sure you won't do that. It's too late anyway.' He shouldered his rifle and, with a mocking wave, sprinted off through the trees.

Several minutes later, she heard the roar of his Jeep. He must have parked up fairly near her car on the dirt road.

She stood, rooted like one of the nearby Douglas firs, her brain whirling. Rufus Stone had put her in a crazy situation. Could she do anything? Should she do anything? Wasn't the confrontation inevitable anyway? It had been boiling up all year from the sound of it. She was a journalist — her job was to record the stark facts. One side wanted to cut down trees, and the other didn't. Apparently there was no room for manoeuvre, or for compromise.

But those tough, young men didn't look like committed conservationists to her. Something sinister was going on. Pete would be at the company office, but where on earth was Rodd Pallister? He was the boss. He should be dealing with this, not swanning around Japan?

Her feet moved. Ellie knew she had to warn Pete. She glanced at her watch. It was half past four. Later than she thought, but the drive back only took half an hour at most. The shift ended at six o'clock, and Pete usually closed up any time from six thirty to nine.

Quickly, she packed up her sketch pad and film, and set off at a dash to the dirt road track. She'd wandered farther than she'd thought, and the undergrowth was dense in places. It took her a good ten minutes to get back to the road, but there was still plenty of time.

At first, she couldn't see her Jeep. She frowned, certain that she'd left it by the clump of hemlock trees. It must be round the next bend. She ran down the hill — it was round the next bend, but considerably farther down the hill, leaning jauntily on its side! The nearside wheels were in a drainage gully at the side of the road. There was no way she could get it out.

Damn Rufus Stone! She didn't need to look in the vehicle to know he'd simply released the hand brake and natural gravity had done the rest.

He hadn't taken any chances, and he'd timed it just right. Salt Creek was five miles away, and there was rough ground to cover. If she was lucky, she'd make it by about six o'clock — which was when the sit-in, or take-over, would happen. There was no way she could warn anyone. It was unlikely anyone would come up the dirt road.

Pete had told Ellie that the loggers would be up in that part in the morning only, and she'd be free to study the bird life in the quiet afternoon. She adjusted her back pack more comfortably on her shoulders, and set off to walk to town.

* * *

Rufus Stone congratulated himself. Operation Hemlock was proceeding exactly as planned.

As he sped down the winding dirt road to the saw-mill, he checked on his operatives on his mobile phone. His right-hand man, Bill Smithers, had despatched a group of genuine conservationists to the north of the island. The ferry had docked, and the consignment of spikes was delivered and en route.

The boys, and a few green people were already in position around the timber yard, waiting for his signal. Ellie Jones was well taken care of. He'd followed her all morning to make sure he relayed the information to her at precisely the right time. She'd arrive in Salt Creek just as the yard was taken over. He wasn't a hundred per cent certain of how she'd react, but it would all help to create the biggest diversionary tactic he'd employed to date.

A couple more coups like this and he'd be able to afford to take things more easily. As for the trees, Pallisters could cut down the whole lot as far as he was concerned. He chuckled to himself. Well, perhaps not yet! They made excellent cover for his real purpose.

The final and most important part of his plan had to be slotted into place. Just outside the town, he drew the Jeep into the side of the road. This phone call needed all his concentration! Besides, there was plenty of time. Just under an hour before Bill would make his move. He dialled the encoded number.

Twenty minutes later he switched off the phone, but didn't immediately restart the Jeep. It wasn't possible! Rufus didn't believe in fate, or coincidence, but if what he'd heard was true, he'd have to have a rethink. So, Ellie

Jones was a complicating factor in the other, main operation. So much the better. There was nothing Rufus Stone liked more than a challenge — especially when there was big money involved! Twice, he went over the information he'd received, and to make sure, jotted down a few notes. Then he turned on the ignition and drove towards the Pallister saw-mill.

Pete Winthrop looked out of his office window. The main day shift had ended, and most of the men had left, mainly by car, but some on foot. A small group chatted near the entrance gates, and three broad-shouldered youths moved towards the office buildings.

'Looks as though they've fallen for it,' he murmured.

The police officer went over to the window and cautiously peered out, standing well back. 'OK, I'll alert the men next door. We won't move until the protesters are actually inside the building. They've closed the gate now, and are putting a chain and padlock on it.

They mean business all right. I just hope all your loggers are off the premises.'

'Most of them. I sent a lot home at lunchtime. I picked out the more — er — volatile ones — for an afternoon off.'

'Well done, Pete.' Rodd, on the other side of the window from the police officer, nodded his appreciation. 'Where's Ellie, by the way. I don't want her involved in this.'

'She's all right. I made sure. I sent her up to Jordan's Creek, bird watching, this afternoon.'

Rodd's body stiffened as he looked out of the window again.

'So what's she doing in the yard? She can't stay there.'

He dashed out, followed by the police officer.

Seconds later, three young men came into the office, demanded the keys, and announced their intention of moving into Pallister's Mill until an undertaking was given not to cut down the trees north of the island.

'You do realise you're trespassing?' Pete said. 'You're here illegally. I give no such undertaking, and I'm asking you to leave.'

'There are plenty more of us outside. And we're here to stay.'

They were belligerent and threatening, but Pete stood his ground. Outside, he saw more protesters gathering, many waving placards. There was no sign of Rodd or Ellie.

Then, a dozen or more off-island policemen, along with Pallister Security Guards, some with dogs, were in the yard. A black van appeared at the gates. One of the guards cut through the chain and swung them back. The police started to round up the crowd. In Pete's office, a couple of policemen, joined the chief officer, swiftly arrested the intruders, and charged them with breaking and entering. Astonished by the ambush, they offered no resistance.

Some scuffles broke out in the yard, but the police cordoned off the protesters, and it was only the young toughies who tried to fight them off. The genuine protesters laid down their banners resignedly, and meekly piled into the awaiting vehicles.

In an hour, the yard was deserted, save for the company Security Guards on night duty, and Pete prepared to close the offices. Rodd had brought a breathless Ellie inside, and the Chief of Police was about to leave.

'That's the last you'll see of that lot. My men are accompanying them on the ferry to Victoria. They'll be dealt with in the courts there. The genuine protesters will probably be bailed, but there are some hard nuts among them — petty criminals who don't give a damn about conserving red cedars or spotted owls. They're a different kettle of fish.'

'Thanks anyway for a highly-efficient operation,' Rodd said and shook the officer's hand.

'Down to you, sir, and Mr Winthrop. I've never seen such a surprised looking mob. How did you do it?'

'Forced them into action by spreading rumours we were going to cut trees up north.' Pete grinned. 'We're not just hick tree fellers you know.'

'Well, you should be able to get on with the job now for a while, but I don't suppose that's the end of it.'

'I'm sure it's not. This issue isn't going to go away overnight.'

Ellie had just about recovered from her final dash into Salt Creek, and her amazement at seeing Rodd. She asked, 'What about Rufus Stone? He set all this up. I didn't see him in the mêlée.'

Rodd and the officer exchanged glances. 'You won't see him in the thick of it, miss. Ever. Keeps well on the sidelines. But he's becoming well-known as a professional agitator.'

'But — '

'Never mind now, Ellie. If we give him enough rope, he's going to hang himself one day. Now, I'm sure you want to be on your way, chief. Thanks again for helping out. Dalton's two police officers couldn't possibly have dealt with this sort of thing. We sure do appreciate the Vancouver Island reinforcements. Pete, Sally'll be anxious. I've got a couple of phone calls to the mainland to make, so I'll close up here.' He stopped Ellie, about to leave with Pete. 'No, not you, Ellie. I want to talk to you — please.'

She shrugged. 'I'll be up for supper later then, Pete. Tell Sally.'

'No,' Rodd repeated. 'I've arranged supper.'

'Where?'

'You'll see. Patience, Ellie.' He smiled at her, and she sat down weakly to wait for him.

9

It was almost dark when they reached a cabin in the forest. Rodd said little during the short drive through the trees, and Ellie was content to wait, now he'd finally returned.

'Too dark for the eagles, I'm afraid. They'll be here at dawn though.' He opened the door and flashed a torch round. 'Wait here, by the door. I'll light the lamps. It's all bottled gas.' The flashing beam weaved about, then suddenly, like a stage set, the room glowed softly to life.

Ellie clasped her hands. 'Rodd, it's lovely!'

'Can be grim in the winter, but once the heaters are on, it's pretty snug. My grandfather built it as a sort of retreat. We've added bits and pieces of comfort.' He smiled. 'Surprisingly, not many people know about it. We're in an ancient forest here — nothing's ever cut down, except for a small clearing round the cabin. Shut the door, and come over here, Ellie.'

He put a match to the log fire laid in the large, stone hearth, stood up, and put his hands on her shoulders. The flames, beginning to leap, reflected in his eyes. Ellie felt the pressure of his fingers. 'I've been worried about you, and when Pete told me you were involved with Rufus Stone — '

'I wasn't! I told you what happened. He found me today — '

'He didn't find you. He'd been following you.'

'But why? And why haven't you been in touch?'

'I couldn't.' He released her. 'Let's eat first, then I'll explain. There's food in the kitchen. I've been living here — this last day or two.' He laid a finger on her lips. 'Food first — and wine — then talk.'

They ate grilled trout, salad, crusty rolls, and drank white wine, which

Rodd set on a low, pine table by a deep sofa. Firelight cast its own gleam over the log walls of the cosy room and, as they finished the meal, Ellie watched the light soften the contours of Rodd's face, and play on the curves of his mouth as he spoke.

'The logging dispute, the protests on Dalton Island, are red herrings — not important compared with what's really going on.'

He laid his arm along the back of the sofa, touching her hair, before he spoke again. 'You know about the drugs problem in Vancouver City — who better than you? It's been spreading to the islands, and now it seems Dalton Island is the latest link in the chain — a potential hand-over point for drugs coming from the East into Canada. There are scores of small islands in the gulf. The drug dealers use one until the police become suspicious, then move on to the next. Dalton's the latest target.'

Ellie was horrified. She'd never even

thought of drugs on the island. It was all so pure, so tranquil, so natural.

'This anti-logging protest alerted us. There was something odd about it, difficult to put a finger on, then one of our contacts put us on to Rufus Stone. He has no police record, but we've discovered he facilitates drug deals and trafficking. His scheme on Dalton Island was to use the logging issue to distract attention from the drugs operations.'

Ellie remembered the smart-suited men in the Cadillac, and told Rodd.

He nodded. 'There's something big coming up. He'd hoped to keep this protest on the boil for days to distract attention from his real purpose. Though this time it's back-fired — he's attracted attention to the island — and underestimated the police network. The tree spikers in the north of the island, by the way, were arrested, too. Dalton will be quiet for a while, and I think the deal will go ahead.'

'Rodd — how do you know all this?'

There was a long pause. Rodd poured more wine, his face sombre. 'I guess I've got to tell you. At the airport, when you were caught, I wasn't there by accident. I — well — I help the drugs squad, as a sort of undercover guy. That's why I knew all about Arthur Smith. That's why I have to lie low here, and why I couldn't come back to the island openly. I had to slip in by boat today to see the ambush — and check you were OK. But Dalton's no longer safe for you any more. We'll have to move you.'

'No! Please, Rodd, I love it here — and I can help you,' she said keenly. 'I can watch Rufus Stone.'

'You most certainly won't. I forbid it absolutely. There are enough problems without having to worry any more about you playing amateur detective.'

'Other problems?'

'The other reason I've been away — Donna.'

Ellie held her breath and Rodd took a sip of wine.

'Donna is the reason I'm committed to helping the drugs squad — in any way I can. You may as well know. Donna is a drug addict. Cathy, my other sister, died of a drug overdose. That killed my father and, after that, my mother committed suicide.' His voice was as cold as a Siberian winter. 'All within the space of two years. All from Amanda's last fling in Europe! She's an addict, too. That's why I helped the police. That's why, when I first saw you, and that case, full of drugs, I was so furiously angry.'

Baldly told facts, but Ellie saw the tension in his body, and the bitterness in his eyes.

'Rodd, I'm so sorry. I'd no idea. You don't still think I — ' In her distress and pity, her voice broke, tears sprang in her eyes and ran freely down her cheeks. 'It's awful,' she sobbed.

He moved closer to her, putting his arms around her. 'Don't cry. No, of course I don't think you're involved. I've come to accept it's over now, and the family's gone, apart from Uncle Ted and Donna. At last she's consented to go to drug rehabilitation clinic. She'd always refused before, but this time she agreed, as long as I stayed with her for the first few days. That's where I've been. Then I had to go to Tokyo on business.'

'Rodd, I can't bear it.' Ellie couldn't stop the tears, and now she knew why. It wasn't just the tragedy of the Pallisters, that was bad enough, but because it was Rodd's family he'd lost, his pain became her pain. She knew she'd fallen in love with him.

She held up her face, and the compassion in her tear-glistened eyes made him tighten his arms round her. For some seconds she clung to him, then as her lips parted, he lowered his head and kissed her.

The kiss was deep and gave her comfort. Ellie felt as if it was she who should be giving comfort, but in spite of his concern for her safety, there was a remote centre in him she couldn't touch. His terrible family tragedy partly explained it. It had turned him into a man with a mission, with little room in his life for personal commitment.

She pushed her hair back, and rubbed her eyes. 'I ought to get back. It's quite late.' Sadness settled glumly round her heart.

'I'll take you now. I've got to be in Vancouver later tonight.' Rodd stood up and cleared the plates and glasses.

'Tonight!'

'I promised Donna. She's at a crucial stage in the treatment. There's hope for her, and I can't let her down. I'll be gone two days, then I'll be back to take you to Corag Island. It belongs to a cousin of mine. There's nothing there except fishing lodges and a few houses. But, for the next two days, you must promise me you'll stay around Sally's. No wandering off in the woods. Rufus Stone will still be on the island.'

'He can't do me any harm, and I've plenty of pictures I still need to take. Eagles at dusk — '

'There are plenty of eagles on Corag Island. Promise me, Ellie.'

She looked rebellious, and Rodd seriously thought about taking her back to Timberlands that night, but Ted was worried about Donna, and spent most of his time at the clinic. Timberlands wasn't safe enough. Besides, apart from Donna, he needed to see the narcotics police in Vancouver City for the latest information.

'Promise,' he repeated.

'All right.' Ellie still thought he was being paranoid about her safety, but she didn't want to add to his problems.

What Rodd didn't tell her was that he'd arranged police protection for her, and also that Arthur Smith had been released on bail, pending his trial in a further eight weeks.

What Rodd wasn't to know was that, two days earlier, Arthur Smith had discreetly forced an entry into Ellie's London flat and, being sharper-witted than the previous operatives, had noted the copies of Conservation Planet's magazines and found letters from that organisation tucked away among the pages. Rodd's blood would have frozen, had he seen the satisfied smile on Arthur Smith's face, as he slipped out of the flat, to make a phone call . . .

Salt Creek was quiet again. The proposed north island logging waited for Rodd's final decision. The rumour of imminent tree felling there had served its purpose in stimulating Rufus Stone to the action which led to the removal of the conservationists. He'd not been seen since the protest, and to Pete's mystification, Rodd had left him on the pay roll.

'I want to know where he is, and what he's doing. If he does come back to collect his pay, let me know at once!'

It was all beyond Pete.

The new bed and breakfast guest Rodd had sent them was a mystery, too. He didn't seem to have a job, but spent an awful lot of time hanging around Ellie, asking questions about wild life on the island.

Ellie was puzzled, too. George Clark was a pleasant enough fellow, but she couldn't get rid of him. And she needed one more session in the forest, filming the eagles at dusk when they were nesting. She felt guilty, but Rodd would never know.

A couple of days after the conservationists' abortive protest, she gave George Clark the slip and took the Jeep, which had been rescued for her by company men, almost to the top of the hillside where she'd found the nesting eagles. She parked quietly, stepped among the trees, and sat down to wait.

It was dusk when the eagles came, winging their way to settle majestically on their high nests. Ellie's camera was ready, focussed, with the special reel of film she always used at dusk. She clicked again and again. The pictures would be perfect. The great birds sat like statues, posed against the dark forest, carved out of their environment. She pressed her button for one last picture, but suddenly all the eagles lifted, and wheeled away from their nests into the sky. Something had disturbed them.

A boat engine! She was on the cliff, just above Hamilton Creek. Her heart leaped with hope. It must be Rodd — he'd come by boat the other evening. Scrambling to her feet, she went towards the cliff edge, and came out on to an open piece of ground directly above the landing stage. It was a boat, quite a large one, but not one she recognised. It moved slowly round the base of the cliff before dropping anchor.

Ellie took out her binoculars, and trained them on the vessel. As she did so, another, smaller boat came in sight. There were no lights on either. It was almost too dark to see, but she could make out bags passed from the larger to the smaller boat. She leaned danger-ously close to the cliff edge, dislodging some loose stones. With a quick reflex, she jerked back.

The men looked up. In the large boat, a solitary figure, well to the stern of the others, saw a pale flash of face and long hair. He guessed it was Ellie, but she had had her glasses trained on the bow, and had missed the unmistakeable, dark pony tail of Rufus Stone. She turned and ran, slithering down the hill, back to the Jeep. She had to tell Rodd.

She should, of course, have gone to Dalton Island's Sergeant Wilkins, but she could only think Rodd must know she was sure she'd seen a drugs drop.

Althea answered the phone at Rodd's Vancouver penthouse. 'Ellie! Good to hear you. Rodd's not in right now. He's — er — with his sister.'

'At the rehab clinic. He's told me about her. Please, Althea, I must get hold of him. It's very urgent. Have you got his number?' She sensed the housekeeper's doubt in the pause. 'Please,' she repeated, 'it's very important.'

'OK.' She reeled off the telephone number realising the seriousness of the situation.

'Thanks.' Ellie's fingers shook as she punched in the number.

The receiver was clamped to her ear, and her hair fell around her face. She didn't see the Jeep come up from the harbour and slowly cruise towards the phone booth and stop. At the same time, George Clark was frantically searching for her on the other side of town.

The nurse in charge was curt. Confidentiality was vital for her clinic's clients, but she promised, with reluctance, to have a word with Mr Pallister — if it was convenient.

Ellie controlled her frustration with difficulty. 'It really is terribly important to reach him,' she pleaded.

'I'll see.'

The wait was agonising as Ellie saw the units on her phone card dwindling. She rummaged in her bag for loose change, then she heard Rodd's voice.

'Ellie?'

'Rodd, thank goodness. I've just seen what I'm sure is a drugs' drop. Out near Hamilton creek.'

'When?'

'Just now. Maybe an hour — not quite'

'Have you told Sergeant Wilkins?'

'No, I thought you — '

'For Pete's sake, Ellie, will you stop being so naïve. I told you not to go into the forest. Where are you now?'

'In a phone booth, near the harbour.'

'Get back to Sally's. Now! Phone the police from there. Find George Clark, and don't leave his side. Got that?'

'What's George Clark got to do with it — '

'Ellie, don't argue. Just do as I say. I'll contact the Vancouver police, and I'll be over as soon as I can. Now, get out of the town and back to Sally's — and stay there!'

'All right. If it's so important.'

'It is. I'll see you soon.'

Ellie replaced the receiver. She wasn't sure whether that was a threat or a promise! Turning to leave the phone booth, she gave a strangled gasp. A pair of dark jeans blocked her way. She shrank back under the glass hood.

'Ellie Jones. Just the person I'm looking for. I see you've got your camera with you. That's handy. I'd like to show you a pretty rare night species.'

'I can't. Not now. I've got to get back to Sally Winthrop's.'

Rufus glanced around. The street was deserted. He took Ellie's arm.

'It won't take long.'

Ellie struggled. 'Let me go. I've told you, I'm not going anywhere with you.'

'It's not far.'

'I've already been out. Just now. There's nothing more I want to see.'

'Ah, it was you on the cliff. Who have you been phoning?'

'None of your business.' She tried to pull her arm away, but Rufus's grip was like iron. She considered screaming, as he pulled her from the phone booth.

He saw what she had in mind and said quietly, in her ear, 'Don't think of it, Ellie. I don't want to hurt you.'

It was impossible to pull away from

him. He clamped her tightly to his side, bundled her quickly into the Jeep, and had started the engine before she could find the door catch. He revved away with such a jerk, Ellie was shot forward, banging her head on the windscreen. Temporarily stunned, she slumped back in the seat.

Rufus smiled. With any luck, it'd keep her quiet until he'd left Salt Creek.

Just after the Jeep left the harbour and disappeared round the bend towards the forest, George Clark's car stopped by the phone booth. He was really getting worried. He hadn't seen Ellie for several hours. Without much hope, he rang Sally Winthrop's. Ellie wasn't there! He got back into his car and drove to the police station.

* * *

In the narcotics section of Vancouver Police Department, the officer on duty took a call from London, his eye on

186

Rodd Pallister, who'd been pacing the room for the past hour, in between making calls himself. The officer listened, and nodded several times. 'Yes. We'll deal with it. Thanks.' He put the phone down.

'Well?' Rodd's eyes flashed with impatience.

'Not good. Our London informant tells us Arthur Smith's lot have found out where Ellie Jones is. Apparently the office at Conservation Planet told them, in all innocence, she was on Dalton Island.'

Another officer came in, acknowledging Rodd, and held out a piece of paper.

'Confirmation — there's to be another drop on Dalton Island tonight, around midnight. A big one. Then they're moving on. Dalton Island's finished now.'

The duty officer stood up. 'OK. The squad's on alert. We can take the custom's cutter. They may not use the same spot twice. We'll leave in half an hour. You'll come with us, Rodd? This is what you've been waiting for — a chance to catch some of the gang red-handed.'

Rodd was already at the door. 'No, I'm going now. I'll fly.'

'They'll hear a sea-plane. It'll scare them off.'

'I'll take that risk. I checked. Ellie isn't at the guest house. Something's happened to her on the island. I'll meet up with you later.'

10

Ellie came to within seconds. They were on a dirt road, among trees. Rufus was flinging the truck round narrow bends. She fastened her seat-belt, and eyed the door catch. A possibility — but if she jumped out — what then?

'Where are you taking me, and what's this rare thing you're going to show me?' Glancing at his hawk-like profile, she wasn't reassured, nor by his mocking laugh.

'It's not so rare a species. Homo sapiens at work under night cover.'

Once he'd delivered the girl, and the drop was made, he'd be off Dalton Island for good. Things hadn't gone too well so far, but he was getting a good price for this particular package. What they did with her was none of his business.

He'd had to re-schedule the midnight

deal to a tiny cove on the other side of the island. He looked at his watch. The boat should be waiting there by now. He turned left to drop down towards the coastline.

They must be a long way from Salt Creek. Travelling through dense forest, Ellie sensed, but couldn't be certain, they were heading north, to the least populated part of the island. The coast there was dangerous; sheer cliffs dropped to rocky inlets with racing drag tides.

'Why don't you tell me what's going on? This is ridiculous. I know your protest didn't work out, but that was nothing to do with me. You made sure I couldn't tell anyone.'

He laughed again, and Ellie's hair prickled.

'I sure did, but I underestimated your friend Pallister, and Pete Winthrop. They've got quite an information network on the island. Knew every move we were going to make, apparently. Trouble is, you know too much, and tonight you've seen too much.'

He stopped the truck, switched off the engine, and came to the passenger side of the vehicle. It was blacker than pitch outside, but Ellie could hear the slap of waves on cliffs and rocks.

'Get out, and don't try anything. There's no way but down — and I've got a gun which, incidentally, I don't mind using. I've nothing to lose now. You're going to meet some interesting homo sapiens, but I'm afraid you're not their favourite person right now.'

One hand gripped her arm, the other held a flashlight, beam pointing downwards. 'See that path, over there. I'm right behind you — start walking.'

Ellie stood her ground. 'Why should I?' she said defiantly.

'Because I say so, and because you've no choice in the matter.'

Ellie stumbled on the rough ground as he pushed her forwards.

'I can drag you, or push you, or you can walk. Just don't give me any more bother.'

Then she was really afraid, both of him and the people who were waiting for her below. She knew that Rodd had been right. Her naïvety had been colossal, and might cost her her life. Whether the earlier drop she'd witnessed had any connection with Arthur Smith she didn't know, but she felt the presence of deadly evil, something far more sinister than anti-logging protests — this was the ultimate horror — drugs — and she was involved up to the hilt!

Terror choked her throat and slowed her feet. Only Rufus Stone, relentlessly prodding from behind, made her move. Her brain seemed to have stopped working.

A night bird called raucously, and the echo sent her mind spinning. Donna! Donna's voice, broken, wrecked. And Rodd's family — because of men like Rufus Stone and those people on the boat. She must put up some sort of a fight. She began to take note of her surroundings. Trees gave way to undergrowth, undergrowth to rocks either

192

side of the path, arching into a tunnel, so low, she had to stoop on all fours.

The rocky passageway ended on a very narrow ledge. Ellie looked down into black water about eight feet below, and across to a dark shape, probably the boat she'd seen earlier! Her hair was gripped from behind, her head pulled painfully back.

'Don't move,' Rufus hissed. 'You'll have us both in the water.' He signalled his torch in a slow arc and almost at once a rubber inflatable moved away from the boat. It carried no light, and was rowed silently towards them.

'What do they want me for?' She tried to turn her head, but his grip was iron.

'They want to interview you about a certain Mr Arthur Smith. You really do have a knack of being at the wrong place at the wrong time. This is where we part company, Ellie. I'm just the delivery man.'

The inflatable bumped against the rock face. The rower shipped oars.

'Have you got her?'

'Sure. Have you got the money?'

'Girl first. Pass her down.'

Ellie knew that once on the boat she'd never have a chance. Rufus Stone came behind her, gripped her armpits and held her over the boat.

The man in the rubber dinghy reached up to grab her feet. She took a huge breath, went limp, then, with all the force of her lungs, gave a loud yell, kicked, twisted sideways, slipped from Rufus Stone's grasp, and fell into the water, filling her lungs with air before she hit the surface. She heard an angry shout, a furious oath from above, then dived deep, kicking off her shoes.

She stayed under as long as she could, swimming away from the ledge. Surfacing very quickly, she had to duck back again as lights swept over the water, both from the ledge, and the boats. Her shout, shattering the silence, had taken Rufus Stone off guard. Ellie had only missed the rubber boat by a fraction, but it had done the trick.

Cautiously, she lifted her head out of the water. There were more shouts as a powerful searchlight from the big boat was switched on. In its light she saw sheer cliffs behind her, then, as the beam passed on, she saw a tiny strip of shingle about half a mile away. She didn't dare make straight for it — it was the only possible landing spot, and they would see that, too.

'I see her. Over there.' It was Rufus Stone's voice.

She dived again, and heard the sound of shooting from the rocks. Underwater, she took off her sweatshirt — it was weighing her down anyway — and released it to the current. Immediately more shots rang out.

A helicopter whirred overhead. As she came up for air, all the boats' lights went out. She heard the noise of a small-engined plane, and in the respite, struck out for the strip of shingle.

Rodd, in his sea-plane, had flown with the unmarked police helicopter, keeping in radio contact. They'd circled the island once. A customs' cutter was on its way from Victoria, followed by one from Vancouver. The information was that it could be a massive haul. Rodd's hands tightened on the controls. For the first time since it had all happened years ago, he had lost sight of his main objective — to help crush drug trafficking. He blamed himself for allowing Ellie to be involved at all.

The radio static crackled. 'Rodd — down there — activity — lights. Damn, they're all out now. Could that be what we're looking for?'

'Could well be. Carry on. With any luck they won't know we've spotted them. Can't see a thing now. Contact the cutters. There's a landing stage just round the headland. I keep a Jeep there. I'll take the plane in.'

'What about the girl? Ellie Jones. Is she back yet?'

'No.' Rodd's voice was grim. 'Just pray to God they don't have her on the boat already.'

Meanwhile, Ellie was crawling up the

shingle. She flopped down, exhausted. The current had been strong, and against her. She sat up, shivering with cold. Out to sea it was quiet, and too dark to make out whether the boat was still there. One thing she was sure of — Rufus Stone would still be in the forest. She just hoped he'd presume her shot, or drowned. She had to try and find a road. Anything was better than sitting in wet clothes on the beach. The cliffs to the right were sheer, but the shingle strip was backed by a gentler slope of wooded hillside. She started to climb through the trees . . .

Rufus Stone was furious. To be out-smarted by that girl! The rubber dinghy had rowed back to the boat as soon as the helicopter had appeared. He hesitated. He should go. His lift to Vancouver would be waiting at Salt Creek, but he had a hunch, and he hated unfinished business. It wouldn't take long. He went back to the truck, and took the track to the small strip of beach he'd seen from the ledge.

The two vehicles nearly crashed head on. Both had been speeding. The truck slewed into a ditch, and Rodd skidded the Jeep to a halt. He recognised the pony tail. Rufus Stone climbed out, but was seized from behind.

'Where is she? Did you take her to the boat?'

Rufus grinned, black eyes glinting evil. 'I tried to, but we didn't quite make it. She's either drowned, or in the woods. It's — '

Rodd's fist swung back and hit the man with such force that the jaw-bone cracked. Before Rufus Stone struck the road, Rodd was back in the Jeep. If Ellie had been in the water, there was only one place she could get out. He hurled the Jeep at top speed towards the woods above the beach . . .

Ellie moved more and more slowly. So tired, all she wanted was to curl up and go to sleep. The earth was so soft . . . just to rest for a second . . . by this tree . . . nice moss . . . she didn't even feel the cold any more. She yawned, thought of Rodd, smiled and fell asleep. She didn't hear the Jeep go by, didn't know she was so near the road . . .

Fur was tickling her. She snuggled near it and put out her hand, then screamed as she saw a huge black bear, on its hind legs, coming for the cub which was playfully examining Ellie.

Rodd had stopped the Jeep to radio back to Salt Creek when he heard the scream. Grabbing his rifle, he ran towards the sound, shouting as he went. He knew there were bears here in the remoter part of the island. They were harmless, if left alone, furious in defence of their cubs.

'Ellie — I'm coming. Don't move.'

She closed her eyes as the bear checked its stride. Shots. The animal dropped on all fours, scooped up her cub, and ran off. Ellie staggered to her feet, held out her hands, and collapsed into Rodd's arms.

He drove her straight to Dalton's tiny hospital, where she was tucked into bed, and made a great fuss of. After initial protests, she succumbed, enjoyed the pampering, and slept the clock round.

When she awoke, both the doctor and Rodd were in the room. Ellie felt oddly shy in her bed in her hospital nightgown.

'Doctor Jansen's given you a complete discharge. No ill effects. You're a brave girl, Ellie.' Rodd's grey eyes smiled his approval. 'I've got his permission to take you on a trip, so if you'll get dressed — '

'I'm not sure I want to go on a trip. The last one was a bit scary.'

'This one'll be different. I promise.'

★ ★ ★

He took her to the log cabin in the woods, and insisted on carrying her from Jeep to sofa.

'I'm not ill, Rodd,' she protested.

'I know that — but — when I think what could have happened!' His face was grim.

'So don't. Just tell me what happened after you took me to the hospital.'

'Mission completed with one hundred per cent success. A huge consignment of drugs retrieved, and some of the real villains rounded up. They should all be in Vancouver jail by now. Along with Rufus Stone, of course.' He frowned, grey eyes holding hers. 'Ellie, why ever did you go with him?'

'I didn't have a lot of choice! But it's not over for me yet, is it? There's the trial — Arthur Smith.'

'He's back on remand. I didn't tell you they let him out on bail. He's the one who found out where you were, and contacted the dealers here. He's implicated now to the hilt, but you'll probably still be needed as a witness.'

'I think I'd better go back to England. I — I'd like to be with my parents. I'll need their help — through the trial.'

'Ah, now, there's a coincidence.' Rodd came to sit by her, and took her hand. 'I brought you here for a purpose, Ellie — a suitable setting for something to ask you.' He paused, as though not quite sure where to start. 'I want to be with you at the trial.'

'You? In London? What about Donna?'

'She's doing fine. Ted'll keep an eye on her. The clinic's doing a great job, weaning her off her dependency on me, as well as tackling the drugs problem.'

'So you'll come to London — just for the trial?'

'Ellie, do I have to spell it out? Don't you know I love you? I can't live without you. When I phoned Sally, and you weren't there . . . ' He shook his head as if unwilling to take the thought any further. 'I'm not risking letting you out of my sight again. I want to marry you — now!'

He pulled her to him and kissed her with tender passion, and Ellie's heart sang its own joy.

'You will marry me, Ellie? I phoned your family this morning, and told your parents I wanted to marry you. They can be at Timberlands in twenty-four hours, and we can be married next week.'

'You spoke to Dad? And Mum?'

'I wanted to know your family, and everything about you.'

'What if I'd said no?' But her eyes denied all possibility of that. They were so full of passionate promise. He had to kiss her again — and again.

'I am so deeply, irrevocably in love with you, Ellie, that I wouldn't have taken no for an answer. I'd have kept you prisoner here until you agreed to marry me.'

'A loving prisoner.'

'I'll build us a splendid home — here on Dalton — or wherever you like.'

'Wherever you are, Rodd. That's where my heart will always be.'

As the eagles soared above them in the blue sky, the lovers, in the log cabin below, sealed their promise to each other in a loving embrace.

VISIONS OF THE HEART

Christine Briscomb

When property developer Connor Grant contracted Natalie Jensen to landscape the grounds of his large country house near Ashley in South Australia, she was ecstatic. But then she discovered he was acquiring — and ripping apart — great swathes of the town. Her own mother's house and the hall where the drama group met were two of his targets. Natalie was desperate to stop Connor's plans — but she also had to fight the powerful attraction flowing between them.

FINGALA, MAID OF RATHAY

Mary Cummins

On his deathbed, Sir James Montgomery of Rathay asks his daughter, Fingala, to swear that she will not honour her marriage contract until her brother Patrick, the new heir, returns from serving the King. Patrick must marry. Rathay must not be left without a mistress. But Patrick has fallen in love with the Lady Catherine Gordon whom the King, James IV, has given in marriage to the young man who claims to be Richard of York, one of the princes in the Tower.

ZABILLET OF THE SNOW

Catherine Darby

For Zabillet, a young peasant girl growing up in the tiny French village of Fromage in the mid-fourteenth century, a respectable marriage is the height of her parents' ambitions for her. But life is changing. Zabillet's love for a handsome shepherd is tested when she is invited to join the La Neige household, where her mistress, Lady Petronella, has plans for her grandson, Benet. And over all broods the horror of the Great Death that claims all whom it touches.

PERILOUS JOURNEY

Caroline Joyce

After the execution of Charles I, Louisa's Royalist father considers it too dangerous for her to stay in England and arranges for her to go to the Isle of Man with Armand de la Tremouille, the nephew of the island's Royalist Governor. Their ship is boarded by Parliamentarians who plan to sail for Ireland, but a storm causes them to be ship-wrecked on the Calf of Man. Magnus Stapleton, the Parliamentarian chief, becomes infatuated with Louisa, but she has fallen in love with Armand.

THE GYPSY'S RETURN

Sara Judge

After the death of her cruel father, Amy Keene's step-brother and step-sister treated her just as badly. Amy had two friends, old Dr. Hilland and the washerwoman, Rosalind, with her fatherless child Becky. When Rosalind falls ill, Amy is entrusted with a letter to be given to Becky on her marriage. When the letter's contents are discovered, it causes Amy both mental and physical suffering and sets the seal of fate upon Rosalind's gypsy friend, Elias Jones.

WEB OF DECEIT

Margaret McDonagh

A good looking man turned up on Louise's doorstep one day, introducing himself as Daniel Kinsella, an Australian friend of her brother-in-law, Greg. He said he had come to stay whilst he did some research — apparently Greg had written to her about it. Louise's initial reaction was to turn him away, but he was very persuasive. However, she was to discover that Daniel had bluffed his way into her life, and soon she found herself caught up in his dangerous mission.